Hold Tight

Gaya Pocker

Contents

01

Jemimah stared at the tall dark handsome guy in front of her blinking her big brown eyes in the process. Ignoring the crowd of guys that had crowded around her and the tomboy who was standing beside him glaring hatefully at her; she took a deep breath closing her eyes and releasing it slowly, lifting her eyelids as well.

"Micah, I want you to listen to me" Jemimah started swallowing her saliva. She needed to say what was deep down in her heart. The things she had buried deeply in her heart never to be exposed to anyone unless she wanted to.

For a long time, she had refused to admit her feelings, she had refused to believe that he was the one. Over and over again, she had assured herself that he wasn't the one, that the tiny squeamish feelings and butterflies she felt will go away. That the comfortable and relaxed feeling she got around him would disappear. That she would treat him like every other one of her guy friends but that didn't happen.

But they didn't, they grew everyday; she believed she was crazy. Of course she was. She couldn't dare to tell anyone. How she fall in love with a cultist?

And not just with an ordinary cultist; the most deadliest of them all No way!

But she did fall in love with him and at this point, Jemimah knew that if she continued to keep or deny these feelings and lock them up; she wouldn't be able to endure them any longer and at a point would be unable to hide it. So today, she had to let him know.

His charcoal black eyes didn't leave her while staring at her quietly. Even as much as he was curious about what she wanted to say; neither his eyes nor his face expressions portrayed his inner thoughts. But her next words did make that perfect sculptured face crack.

"I like you" Jemimah said shaking her head and throwing her arms up in the air.

"I sound crazy, I know. I know that I sound super crazy or rather I am crazy. To be honest; for a while I refused to admit it. That I fell in love with a cultist, that I fell in love with you. I refused to believe it. I mean you....." Jemimah paused thinking for the right words to say while throwing her arms up in the air and then letting them drop limply beside her and then raising her head to look to meet his coffee brown eyes again.

"But then I realized something; that whether you are a cultist or not; you are just you. You are just Micah" Jemimah said her face expressions further explaining her words and thoughts.

"I'll be sincere and honest Micah; I don't know what tomorrow holds for you; what tomorrow holds for me or what it holds for you and me but there's one thing I know and I'm sure of. That I want to be with you" Jemimah added sighing.

"I love you Micah" Jemimah added softly.

Never in her life did Jemimah imagine that she would say such words to someone. That 'someone' could have been anyone but Obaniyi Micah was so out of the equation.

Two months ago, if someone had told her she would say such words to him; she would have vehemently disagreed with such a person. But here was she saying those very words.

Two months ago, she would shiver and take to her heels upon hearing his name. She would get panic attacks when in the same space with him.

Two months well.........

TWO MONTHS AGO

Jemimah yawned as soon as the PHY 101 lecturer packed his notes and walked out of the class. Running her eyes over her note and the few points she had jotted down; she made a mental note to ask her brother about his own note else; Jemimah was sure she would be chewing her biro in the test hall. She grabbed the pen recorder beside her and turned it off.

The Lecture theater was quick to turn rowdy and noisy as the students stood up and started exiting the hall. Knowing fully well that any of their lecturers could go bonkers and decided to fix a class the next minute, she packed her books into her tote bag; draping it over her shoulder as she walked out of the hall.

The sun seemed to wanted to pick a fight with Jemimah began the terrifying sun rays that descended upon her as soon as she walked out made her run towards the trees beside the theatre hall while squinting her eyes at the sun.

She brought out her phone from her bag and scrolled through her messages opening her departmental group chat for any messages for lecture updates and just as Jemimah thought, one of their lectures had gone bonkers.

"What's wrong with this man now? How he dey take change location like this nah?"

"Wasn't his class until tomorrow?"

"Why these people like to do dey do us like this?"

"I no dey go, I dey go my hostel abeg"

"You no go attend Bayode's class, e be like say you wan carry over this course abi"

The conversation of some of her departmental mates who were standing few meters away from Jemimah drifted into her ears and she couldn't help but roll her eyes. Pouting her lips and glaring at the sun, she started walking towards the lecture theater where the lecture was supposed to take place.

Its had been three months and half since she resumed into Crest University Akure. A big, popular private university. Public-private so to say. Although they paid exorbitant fees like other private universities; they were as populated as other public universities. In her three month and half stay; Jemimah only had one word for the school.

Boring.

When she had gotten admission; Jeremiah had been relay excited and for days and days couldn't stop talking about CUA the school for her and she couldn't wait to resume school. But upon resumption, Jemimah had found the school really boring; except for the occasional cult clashes and the huge school forum which always had interesting news and latest updates; nothing interested her.

What was more; making friends suddenly became a problem for Jemimah. As none of her best friends from secondary school had chosen CUA; she had to make new friends but Jemimah? She had none. She vividly remembered the first Faculty and Departmental meeting with the 100 level students.

Everyone was new and curious, excited to start school and make friends. before the meeting ended, a lot of the students had started talking to each other laughing and making small talk while Jemimah was left alone looking like an alien.

Bimbo was the only other person from Boston International College that came to Boston. why she had come was obvious. they weren't in the same department or Faculty so Jemimah had slowly found herself being accustomed to be alone all the time.

The sun seemed hell bent on picking a fight with Jemimah and she soon realized that her blouse was already sticking to her back with beads of sweat running down her back. she walked towards one of the many scattered student kiosks and got herself a drink. Sipping the cold Fanta that brought a kind of calm to Jemimah's nerves and body.

"Jemimah!" Someone called and Jemimah turned a smile crawling up her lips the moment she came face to face with the person who had called her.

"Bimmy, what's up?" Jemimah greeted as latter also approached the kiosk to get herself a drink.

"I'm fine. What are you doing here? Isn't your lecture at Adejuye LT?" Bimbo asked and Jemimah shrugged.

"That man is a sadist. We have days on when he teaches but I want to believe that something keeps sticking up his ass so changes locations and date every single time" Jemimah replied and Bimbo bent over her legs laughing.

"We are just finished ours. I'm done for the day" Bimbo informed Jemimah while the latter hissed folding the straw into the bottle and covering the drink.

"Lucky you. After this; I still have one more. Just cook ehn; I'm late for class already" Jemimah said and Bimbo rubbed her back laughing.

"Just order for food. I have things to do and I and Jeremiah have somewhere to go. I might get back to the hostel late at night" Bimbo said and Jemimah nodded.

"Okay then. Bye bye" Jemimah said as she waved at Bimbo as she continued walking towards her destination. She sipped her drink while walking since she had no one to talk to till she got to the already rowdy and noisy hall. She stepped into the lecture theater while scanning for the available seats and scrolling through her phone. Messages like the Class President saying that the man suddenly had an emergency and couldn't make it to the class was a message that Jemimah was seriously praying would pop up on her screen.

Rummaging through her bag; she brought out her Air pods and fixed into her ears trying to block out the noise and the conversations of the three girls seated in front of her.

It had always been like that. While other students and their friends sat down talking and gossiping about god knows what; she had no one but her phone to turn to. For someone who everyone wanted to be friends with in secondary school; then coming to university and turning to a loner was out of it was an irony that would make any laugh and cackle. Jemimah curled her lips upwards while shaking her head.

How ironic.

Knowing fully well that the lecturer would take time before appearing for the class even if he was the one who fixed a last minute class; she opened her VLC and continued watching one of the movies she had been watching the night before.

Barely she had the movie been playing for more than a minute when Jemimah felt someone tapping her shoulder. She paused the movie and turned to see a girl smiling at her. She removed one of her Air pods seeing the girl's lips move.

"Is anyone seated here?" She asked and Jemimah shook her head. She then watched the girl turn and call someone over.

"Paul! Peter! There's space here" the girl said and Jemimah quietly slipped her Air pods back into her ears wondering why there was someone who wanted to seat beside her. She had always had space beside her in lecture halls, even when there were people seated beside her; both parties always treated each other as if they didn't exist.

She watched as two guys approached before she blinked her eyes in a daze. Both of them were exact replicas of each other. If it had been at night; Jemimah would have confirmed that she was seeing double . Remembering the names the girl had called them earlier, she figured out they were twins. Apart from the fact that they were twins and exact replicas of each other, Jemimah had to admit that they were both good looking. The girl sat down beside her and the twins also sat down. Jemimah returned to her movie as the girl tapped her again.

"Is there a problem?" Jemimah asked removing one of her ear pods again.

"You are Jemimah right?" She asked and Jemimah nodded not surprised a bit that the unfamiliar looking girl knew her.

"Yeah. A problem?" Jemimah asked again and the girl shook her head.

"Adeyemi Doyinsola, nice to meet you" she replied with a smile while Jemimah looked at her like she had grown three heads before nodding her head nodded.

"Same here Doyin" Jemimah said offering her a smile.

"This is Paul and Peter" Doyin introduced with a grin.

"You can call them P square" Doyin added laughing at her own joke and Jemimah nodded.

"Hello, Paul" one of the guys said introduced smiling at Jemimah.

"Peter" the other one said and Jemimah smiled waving as well.

"Nice to meet you P square" Jemimah said and Paul laughed.

"Its actually a stupid name so I'll prefer if you don't call us that" Peter said and Jemimah raised her eyebrow.

"When your friend first suggested that I called you that, you could have clearly refuted her and ask that I do not address you like that. You didn't have to wait till I called you that and make me feel stupid" Jemimah replied already irritated by the trio.

She immediately turned and slipped her Air pods back into her ears and barely two minutes later; the lecturer walked in. Throughout the class; Jemimah discovered that she was in a foul mood. She would miss some spellings and mix some words together and even forget some words in the middle of the dictation. The fact that the trio sat beside seemed to irritate her more and by the time the class was ending; Jemimah wanted nothing more than to crash into her bed.

When the Class President directly announced that the next class had been rescheduled till the next day; Jemimah wanted to moan out of excitement. She was tired and famished.

She packed her books back into her bag and stood up to leave the hall when Doyin stood up to talk to her. Jemimah raised an eyebrow at her shutting the other girl who had already opened her mouth up as she made way for her to pass. Jemimah chuckled wondering what she wanted to say.

Apologize?

She caused it either ways. If she hadn't suggested that she called them P square, there was no way she would have called them such a stupid though hilarious name. It was only right she apologized but she honestly didn't want to hear it.

"Jemimah" someone called and Jemimah turned to see one of the twins flashing her a smile. She honestly couldn't differentiate in between

"Peter can be very sensitive sometimes; I hope you don't mind" Paul said and Jemimah chuckled.

"Well I do mind" Jemimah replied walking away twice as irritated as she was before.

"Why did you say that earlier?" Doyin asked and Peter slipped his hands into his pockets shrugging his shoulders.

"It was rude and unpleasant" Doyin added.

"I know" Peter said and Doyin threw up her hands in the air.

"What?" Peter asked.

"Go and apologize to her right now!" Doyin replied while Peter furrowed his brows.

"Well that's not going to happen" Peter said and Doyin folded her arms.

"You can as well forget about the whole spaghetti thing" Doyin said and Peter stared at her in disbelief.

"Doyin!" He called out and Doyin shrugged.

"Its boring been the only girl with you two. I really like Jemi but you annoyed her already" Doyin replied and Paul chuckled.

"I don't think she's going to like that nickname" Paul said while Peter nodded.

"My thoughts exactly. And besides you want to be friends with a stuck-up and arrogant girl like her?" Peter asked.

"You've met and even though you annoyed her; in that brief moment you and I will admit that she's not like what the rumors say" Doyin replied

"So why doesn't she have any friend?" Peter asked and Doyin shrugged.

"That's not my business and besides I am now her friend. So go and apologize to her, no one does that to my friend and goes scot free" Doyin replied and Paul burst into laughter at Peter's crestfallen expression.

"Doyinsola, I know you don't mean that" Peter said and Doyin curled up her lips.

"Well I mean every single word" Doyin said pushing Peter towards the door.

"Now off you go" Doyin said while Peter turned to glance at her.

"Don't look at me, go and apologize already" Doyin said pushing him away with her hands. Rolling his eyes, he jogged down the stairs to look for the girl who apparently had disappeared.

Jemimah pouted as her phone rang and she saw the caller ID. She picked the call while adjusting the ear pods in her ears.

"Heyy" Jemimah greeted and Jeremiah's voice drifted into her ears.

"What's up? Done with classes?" Jeremiah asked while Jemimah yawned a little.

"Yeah. My last class got postponed. I'm on my way to my hostel now" Jemimah replied.

"Bimbo and I are heading out later. Do you want to come?" Jeremiah asked and Jemimah snorted.

"Comer ni. You want me to come and be a third wheel. Nah I'll pass. You two have fun" Jemimah replied ending the call.

02 ' TWO '

- -

Jemimah rubbed her forehead slipping her phone back into her bag. She was so done been the third wheel at Jeremiah and Bimbo's dates. She of course enjoyed being with her elder brother and her only friend in school but she definitely didn't enjoy been the third wheel.

She adjusted her bag on her shoulder when suddenly a tall shadow loomed over her and Jemimah raised her head to see who was standing in front of her. She rolled her eyes and moved to walk away and the shadow was twice as quick as her to block her way.

"What do you want?" Jemimah asked bored.

"I'm sorry" Peter replied and Jemimah turned to him in slight surprise.

"I'm sorry about earlier. It was rude and insensitive of me" Peter added while Jemimah squinted her eyes at him.

"Doyin told you to apologize huh?" Jemimah asked watching as Peter's brows lifted up in surprise.

"You don't have to do things you don't want to do because of others. Most especially, you don't have to apologize to anyone if you are not been honest about it" Jemimah added not waiting for Peter's reply before turning and walking away.

Maybe because she had already gotten used to her loner life, Jemimah wasn't in the bit bothered that while a lot of the students were clustered together talking loudly and chattering with excitement all over their faces; she had her bag to hold and her ear pods playing music to keep her comfort. She couldn't even talk to herself.

Jemimah sighed as she turned into the lane of her hostel. The day was once again ending without anything new or anything special.

"Jemi!" Someone yelled and subconsciously Jemimah turned to see Doyin running towards her. Puzzled and confused, her steps came to a stop as she watched the dark skinned girl run towards her.

"So what did she say?" Doyin asked as she intertwined her hands with Peter's.

"Doyin told you to apologize right? You don't have to do things you don't want to do because of others. Most especially, you don't have to apologize to anyone if you are not being honest about it" Peter replied as Paul and Doyin stared at him confused.

"What is that?" Paul asked.

"I'm not following, what are you saying?" Doyin asked.

"That's what she said" Peter replied and he slid his hands into his pockets.

"Wow" Paul said after a while scratching the back of the head.

"You two had better follow me" Doyin said as she started running.

"Doyin where are you running to?" Paul yelled after her jogging after her.

"Stop running, what if you trip?" Peter yelled after her as he also started running after her.

Doyin tried to regulate her breathing as she stood in front of Jemimah who was still wearing a confused and surprised look.

"Heyy" Doyin said after a while and Jemimah nodded.

"Why did you run after me?" Jemimah asked and Doyin sighed straightening up. She didn't know why or what must have caused it but ever since she saw Jemimah in the lecture theater; the urge to get close to this rumored stuck up and arrogant girl had been too overwhelming.

She couldn't figure out why or how she was feeling that way but she did want to get close to her. She was really curious about her. The twins as well had caught up to her and Doyin smiled at Jemimah.

"I met the Paul and Peter at Summer lesson in my SSS2. We weren't going to the same school but we've been friends since then. Three years and counting, so I know them quite a bit" Doyin started and Jemimah nodded wondering where the conversation was going.

"Okayyyyy" Jemimah replied dragging the y to tell Doyin she still didn't understand why or the reason for the information.

"And one thing I'll tell you is this, Paul could do anything for anyone at all even if he has to go out of his comfort zone, he really wouldn't mind but Peter? Nah, he's so far one of the most selfish people I've met in my life. You have to be at a particular level in Peter's heart for him to leave his comfort zone for you, he absolutely wouldn't do something if he doesn't want to. Never, he wouldn't" Doyin added as Jemimah blinked her eyes genuinely surprised.

"I'm sorry" Peter said again and Jemimah nodded pursing her lips.

"Its okay" Jemimah replied and Doyin stretched out her hands towards her.

"Friends?" Doyin asked and Paul laughed.

"Doyin this is old school" Paul said while Peter burst into laughter while a small smile tugged at Jemimah's lips.

"I like old school, you have a problem?" Doyin asked pouting and Jemimah laughed lightly as she took Doyin's hand.

"Friends" Jemimah replied wearing a small smile.

"Girlllll, you really should smile more. You look hot everyday but you absolutely look breathtaking when you smile" Doyin said and Jemimah laughed.

"Thank you"

"What's your room number?" Doyin asked as they climbed the stairs into the hostel. Paul and Peter had gone to their hostel which was just before theirs.

"128" Jemimah replied and Doyin nodded turning the opposite way.

"I'm coming" she said to Jemimah and the latter nodded watching as she as she disappeared down the corridor.

Jemimah was sure she always spent between ten to fifteen minutes walking to the hostel. She walked slowly and at her own pace but that evening, it felt like it was a three-minute walk even if she had no idea if the world clock was fast forward or if they were the ones who had walked faster.

Jemimah climbed the staircase slowly and walked towards the room on the left before slowly pushing the door open. Her room was three rooms away from the staircase. The room was noisy as usual with the other three girls chattering loudly and laughing. None of them seemed to pay attention to Jemimah as she walked inside the room; not that the latter valued their attention.

She sat down on her bed ad she pried off her bag off her shoulder before slowly removing her sandals and wearing her palm slippers.

"So wait, in summary, he just wanted to collect Vickie's number?" one of the girls asked smacking the gum in her mouth

"Ehn now. The stupid boy was now using the excuse if having his departmental mates number as an excuse" another girl replied.

"I heard his parents are rich though" the first girl said again.

"Who wants his money?" The girl seating on the bed opposite Jemimah asked as she hissed getting down from the bed and walked towards the wardrobe in front of the bunk.

The caramel skinned girl had a flawless skin and a lean body which swayed as she walked towards the wardrobe. Her face was devoid of pimples or rashes and her eyes seemed to shine naturally. As she bent down to retrieve something from her wardrobe, her braids fell against her shoulders exposing the tiny collarbones after her neck.

Bringing out three packets of chocolates, she walked back to the bed throwing the remaining two girls the two chocolates.

"Thank you Vickie's. Is this not the chocolate we saw Cynthia and her friends eating that day? The one she said her brother worked in? The one in Canada?" the first girl asked again and Victoria nodded.

"Its imported" she replied nonchalantly but there was no mistaking of the pride in her voice.

If there were people who irritated her the most in CUA, then it was Jemimah's roommates. Each room had four occupants with giants wardrobe enough to occupy your clothes and other materials. There was also space for a reading table and chair each and at the end of the room was the bathroom. Opposite the the door was another smaller than enclosed of a small sizeable space where the girls could cook and do their kitchen activities.

When they all had all resumed, none of the girls had talked to each other. Each doing their things as if others didn't exist. Jemimah had gone for class one day and came back to meet the three other girls chattering and fawning over one of them. It then became the trio acting like she didn't exist at all.

Jemimah rubbed her stomach seriously hunger washing over her like tidal waves. She hissed quietly pondering on whether to order for food or to cook. Either ways, she had to wait till the food got done or wait for two or one hour before she food gets delivered. She should have gone with Jeremiah and Bimbo for their date at least, she wouldn't be hungry.

None of the choices appealed to Jemimah at all. She stood up from her bed peeling off the jean trousers from her legs and folding it neatly on her bed. She walked towards her wardrobe and changed into a pair of jeans shorts and draped a big faded round neck on it.

Even the none of boxes of cheese balls, caprisonne, yoghurt, biscuits, chocolates and snacks that Jemimah had, piled up in her wardrobe appealed to her. A box of chocolate exactly like what the other girls in the room were eating was placed in Jemima's locker. Jemima's stomach rumbled lightly and Jemima found herself laughing at her stomach. There was a knock on the door and everyone turned towards the door.

"Come in" one of the girls said as the door opened and Doyin walked in.

"Oh hello" Doyin said smiling when she saw Jemima

"I almost thought I was lost" Doyin said and Jemima chuckled.

"Seat down nah. That's my bed" Jemima said pointing chuckling while the other three girls stared in surprise and shock.

Not that Jemima could blame them. In her one month stay, unlike others, no one had ever come to look for her in her room except Bimbo. No one, no one at all. Jemima sat down beside Doyin on the bed who was looking around the room.

"You guys are so neat. You need to meet my roommates, they are the queens of roughness. Me not excluded though" Doyin said and Jemima laughed quietly her stomach following her lead in rumbling again.

"You haven't eaten?" Doyin asked laughing at her rumbling stomach.

"I'm tired. Cooking anything except noodles will take at least thirty minutes, ordering for food will have me waiting for maybe an hour before the food gets delivered, neither works for me" Jemima replied falling on her bed and almost immediately Doyin grabbed her hand pulling her up.

"Let's go to my room" Doyin said pulling the latter with her as they walked out of the room.

"You are also on this floor?" Jemima asked.

"I thought your room was downstairs" Jemima added as Doyin opened the door of a room down the corridor.

"No o. I wanted to collect something from someone" Doyin said pulling Jemima into the room and the noisy chatter in the room came to a stop.

Jemima had never been to someone's else room except Bimbo and it was on very few occasions. She preferred to remain her room all alone and bored. It was her first time entering a room that wasn't hers or Bimbo's.

"You people, this is my new friend, Jemima" Doyin introduced as the girls waved at Jemima.

"Hello" Jemima said softly pursing her lips.

"Jemima right?" One of the girls asked and Jemima nodded.

"Its you" the girl said again and Jemima chuckled while Doyin frowned her face.

"Don't say its you and start making her feel awkward. Weren't you guys talking about cult groups? Then continue, stop embarrassing my friend" Doyin said pulling Jemima to seat down on her bed.

Jemima definitely knew what sweetness felt like but in that minute as Doyin spoke up for her, Jemima knew she hadn't felt that sweet in a long while. It was a lingering sweet feeling that she even wanted to linger more but it was soon gone twice as slow as it came though.

Doyin walked into the small kitchen at the edge of the room while Jemimah was left to explore the room. She had been so right abut she and her roommates being queens of roughness, the room was clean in every sense but there were sandals and slippers littered everywhere, almost every bed in the room had piles of unfolded clothes that Jemimah was double sure had unwashed and dirty clothes mixed with them. Doyin's bed not excluded. The beds were all unmade and two of the wardrobes were scattered. Jemima wanted to laugh but she ended up smiling. the rooms were rough but it had a feeling of homely that her her ever clean and conspicuous room could never have.

Doyin stepped out of the kitchen placing a plate of spaghetti in her hands. She placed the plate in Doyin's hands wearing a menacing face as she spoke.

"Don't even think of rejecting it" Doyin said pushing the unfolded clothes to the edge of the bed to make space for her.

"If you aren't full, take more o" Doyin said as she crossed her legs on the bed.

Jemima nodded her head digging into the food. the jollof spaghetti was peperish but it was exactly what she needed. Throwing her pride to the side, she finished the plate of spaghetti and didn't even realize when she had walked into the kitchen and gave herself another helping of spaghetti on her plate and started eating again.

"You seem really hungry" Doyin said laughing as she continued chattering to Jemima who listened carefully at every word she was saying.

The sun had gone down and what was left was the orange and red skies. The day was ending and it was still a normal usual day except that few hours ago, Jemima had thought her day was going to end as usual and few hours later; it was ending with her having friends.

As Doyin said a joke that sent her laughing whole heartedly, Jemima was sure that her day wasn't ending the usual way.

03 'THREE'

"Honestly, I would choose Wizkid over Davido anytime, any day" Doyin said and Paul hissed.

"Who Wizkid epp? Guy, do you realize that Davido and Wizkid aren't on the same level?" Paul asked.

"That's a fact. Davido is not on the same level with Wizkid nah. Who doesn't know?" Doyin asked while Jemima laughed lightly.

"Me I don't understand why you guys are arguing or anything. Both artistes don't know you and its not as if they more you argue the more you get money" Peter said receiving a glare from Doyin.

"Is it your mouth we are using to argue? What's your own?" Doyin asked while Jemima and Paul burst into laughter.

"You have problem" Peter said shaking his head.

"Did you hear?" Doyin asked bending her head and whispering all of a sudden while Jemima furrowed her brows.

"That what?" She asked as her phone started ringing. A soft smile crawled on her face as she picked the call.

"Heyy J" Jemima said into the phone.

"What's up? Where are you?" Jeremiah asked and Jemima pouted.

"I'm in President Muritala Lecture Hall" Jemima replied.

"I'm right outside. C'mon out" Jeremiah replied and Jemima turned towards the entrance door of the lecture hall catching his figure almost immediately. She dropped the phone in her hand and got to her feet.

"My elder brother is outside, wanna meet him?" Jemima asked carefully.

It had only been two days since she became friends with these people and they weren't just the best of the best but Jemima could swear they were the best days she had, had so far in CUA.

"Of course I want to. I've only heard about your brother. Never seen him close before. Let's go and meet your handsome brother" Doyin replied getting to her feet and rushing after Jemima who laughed walking outside the hall.

Jeremiah was standing outside with his hands in his pockets. Clad in a pair of jeans and a white sneakers; he donned a plain white tee and jeans jacket.

"Whawooo" Doyin whispered beside Jemima who chuckled silently.

Jemima instantly hugged Jeremiah as soon as she got to him while the latter dropped a peck on her forehead.

"How you doing lil sis?" Jeremiah asked with a small smile. He of course knew how lonely and friendless his sister was. He knew her predicament more than anyone else.

"Fine" Jemima answered honestly and as Jeremiah opened his mouth to say something, he noticed the three students standing behind his younger sister.

"Hello" Jeremiah greeted politely as he turned to Jemima.

"This is Doyin, Paul and Peter.... " Jemima said answering Jeremiah unasked question taking a small pause before smiling.

"My friends" Jemima finished as a look of surprise flashed through Jeremiah's eyes before he also smiled lightly.

"Hello, nice to meet you. Jeremiah" Jeremiah introduced himself immediately.

"Hello, you look handsome in person" Doyin said earning a chuckle from him.

"Thank you" he said slapping handshakes with the twins before grabbing his younger sister's hand and turning to the trio.

"I'll be borrowing your friend for the rest of the day. Sorry" Jeremiah said and the twins laughed.

"No worries" Paul replied while Jemima waved at her friends allowing Jeremiah to pull her away.

"Where are we going?" Jemima asked and Jeremiah shrugged.

"Somewhere" Jeremiah replied as he chuckled and walked towards a black Prada parked beside the road. Jemima walked towards the front passenger seat and got in after Jeremiah.

"And who owns this?" Jemima asked as Jeremiah darted her a glance not replying before igniting the engine and driving away.

"So you decided to bring me on a date out of the blues?" Jemima asked with a snort scooping her ice cream into her mouth while Jeremiah shrugged.

"Just felt like" Jeremiah replied as he took a bite out of his meat pie.

"So....... you cool?" Jeremiah asked as Jemima went silent. She didn't reply or say anything till she finished her cup of ice cream. She placed the empty paper cup on the table and ran her tongue over her lips wiping every bit of stain that might have left on her lips.

"I want more ice cream" Jemima replied while Jeremiah chuckled before standing up and walking towards the counter to get more ice cream. He came back with a bigger cup of ice cream and placed it in front of Jemima.

"I am fine honestly" Jemima said with a small smile.

"The last two days..... " Jemima started as she took a small pause.

"It was fun" Jemima finished and Jeremiah laid back on his seat with a small smile.

Since Jemima had resumed to CUA, she only had a word for the University. Boring. She had said it repeatedly and repeatedly that he stopped asking her.

"Doyin, Paul and Peter?" Jeremiah asked quietly and Jemima nodded.

"They are certainly not like Farouq, Faidat, Adesewa and Kamfah but they are fun. Doyin been cooking for the both of us for the past two days" Jemima replied and Jeremiah laughed softly.

"You turned her to your cook already?" Jeremiah asked in a joking tone.

"She likes cooking" Jemima instantly defended herself while Jeremiah laughed heartily nodding.

"Then its fine" Jeremiah said and Jemima smiled and continued eating her ice cream.

Many a time, Jemima had always thought about her lucky she was. She of course knew how worried Jeremiah was about her. She did know that he and Bimbo always brought her on their dates not because they liked having a third party around but it was to make her feel less lonely and not to feel left out.

"Babe" a familiar voice rang near Jemimah's ears as she turned and snorted at Bimbo.

"When have you been ehn?" Jemima asked watching as Bimbo reached over to Jeremiah and dropped a peck on his cheeks before seating down.

"My classes have been tight, sorry I couldn't come to your room" Bimbo replied while Jemima nodded and yawned.

"I'm tired so I'll leave your two alone" Jemima replied grabbing her bag and standing up.

"Where are you going?" Jeremiah asked in surprise and Jemima snorted at him.

"Nowadays, I hate been a third party more than anything" Jemima replied closing the distance between the two and dropped a peck on their cheeks and walked out of the restaurant before they could say anything else.

Jemima checked her wristwatch as soon as she stepped out of the restaurant. It just a few minutes past 4pm. She did really hate been a third party and for some weird reason it was beginning to irritate her. Maybe she didn't mind or care when she was in secondary school when all her friends got boyfriends and crushes and she was all alone.

But now things were different. Not that Jemima knew what was different though. Not really was different though. Been fed with dog food from almost every couple wasn't a new thing but Jemima had realized that whenever she was around Jeremiah and Bimbo, it was a constant reminder of how lonely she was and her heart would always feel twice as empty as usual.

Jemima didn't have a specific type of guy. Call it impossible or crazy but Jemima had not even crushed on someone before. Never in her life had she given a guy more than two glances. Not that they weren't attractive enough or anything but none of them absolutely interested her.

It was a feeling Jemima hadn't had in a very long time but she did want someone she could easily talk to, someone she maybe liked. Someone she could show herself to without wondering if he would find her weird or not. She really did want to like someone but she couldn't force herself to like someone could she? she actually wanted someone she could call her own person.

Jemima chuckled at her childish thinking shaking her head and coming to a stop by the road side while waiting for a bike to board back to the school gates. A red sports car suddenly rolled to a stop beside her and Jemima watched with her eyebrows raised.

"Jemima right?" The guy asked and Jemima raised her eyebrow at the guy who was asking her a question. the fact he was clad in black overalls and a black face mask made her face wrinkle.

"Yeah?" Jemima replied watching as his lips pulled into a small smile.

"Hop in. Jeremiah asked me to drop you off at school" He replied and Jemimah felt her phone buzz in her hands. She rolled her eyes before swiping the call button and pressing the phone to her ears.

"Have you seen Black?" Jeremiah asked.

"Black?" Jemima asked as the guy nodded retaining his smile.

"Yeah" Jeremiah replied.

"Jemima" Jeremiah called and Jemima sighed.

"Huh?" Jemima replied as a soft sigh from Jeremiah drifted into her ears..

"You are not a third party" Jeremiah replied and Jemima smiled before ending the call. She threw Black another look before opening the door and getting into the car.

"Want me to close the partition?" Black asked as soon as they got back to the road.

Jemima stared at the open space car and at the kind of looks everyone else was giving them. A sports car and a red colored one at that was bound for attention. And that attention, Jemima was tired of it.

"Yes please" she replied and Black nodded his hands reaching for the partition button. the wind blew against Jemima's face, her emotions calming down in an heartbeat. One of her hands shot out and held Black's and the other guy turned to her in surprise.

"On the other hand, just leave it" Jemima said swallowing his saliva and letting go of his hand.

"You like the wind?" He asked and Jemima turned to him in slight surprise before nodding.

"Yes" she replied and Black stretched his hand out against but this time around it was to increase the volume of the music. His phone rang almost the same time he increased the volume. His smiling face was immediately replaced a blank face the moment he glanced at his phone while Jemima watched him interesting. He immediately stopped the music while picking the call.

"King" Black called as he slowly removed his foot from the accelerator.

"Pick Toni up on your way back" a deep voice reverberated through the call and Jemima suddenly got goosebumps.

"Okay" Black replied taking a short pause.

"King" he called hesitantly.

"Huh?" The latter replied.

"Professor Farida wanted to see you" Black replied and Jemima furrowed her eyebrows. After a long pause, the voice rang in Jemimah's ears again.

"No worries" the latter replied and the call ended. The music continued playing and Jemima found herself taking notice of features she hadn't noticed before.

Except for the black overalls that she had noticed before and his hair been covered with a black face cap; his fingers were adorned with different rings and there a small tattoo peeking out of his wrist . And she also realized a fact she had noticed before, he was really cute.

The voice that had given Jemima goosebumps earlier seem to ring in Jemima's mind again and she chuckled and swallowed her saliva. To think that there was a human with a voice that could give her goosebumps.

Jemima didn't remember deep voices being her thing at all but hearing the so called King's voice; she was seriously thinking of putting it her Things I Want in a Man. He has to have a deep voice.

"You are in what Faculty?" Black asked as they drove into the school.

"Faculty of Medical Sciences" Jemima replied.

"What about you?" Jemima asked.

"Faculty of Management Studies. Accounting actually" Black replied and Jemima raised her eyebrows in surprise.

"Wow" Jemima muttered folding her arms.

"Why? I don't look that smart?" Black asked laughing and Jemima shook her head.

"Not exactly. You look like someone who might be in Theatre Arts or something" Jemima replied honestly.

"Because of my rings?" Black asked again waving his hands while Jemima laughed.

"Maybe" Jemima replied nodding her head.

"You aren't in 200 level are you?" Jemima asked again and Black shook his head.

"No, I'm not. 300 level" Black replied.

"So how did you know my brother?" Jemima asked and Black laughed.

"Maybe no one told you but your brother was twice as popular as he is now when he was a fresher. I met through King though" Black replied as Jemima pursed her lips.

"King? The one who called a few minutes ago?" Jemima asked and Black nodded.

"Yeah" Black replied as the car came to a stop.

"Sorry, I have to pick someone up" Black said and Jemima nodded. she had clearly heard King telling him to pick someone up. she looked around and found a group of people clustered together and shouting on top of their voices.

"Are they fighting?" Jemima asked with a small frown but her eyes widened in surprise as Black flew out of the car flawlessly and started walking towards the group of people with a visible scowl on his face. His cute face was furious as he walked and Jemima could feel chills down her spine.

She blinked her big brown eyes watching as Black tapped one of the guys and the expressions of the guys changed at once. Jemima furrowed her brows seeing the expressions on the guys shouting change and they went quiet as Black started saying things she couldn't hear.

"Wait, are they scared or what?" Jemima asked laughing quietly. She had no idea what he must have said but he soon turned and started walking towards the car while a guy followed him. the guy looked like he had been roughened and Jemima realized that the guy had a small cut on his lips as they neared.

They were beating him up?

The guy seemed surprised seeing Jemima in the front seat as he turned to Black.

"Jerry's sister" Black replied flying into the driver's seat exactly the way he flew out.

"You good?" Black asked turning towards the new guy who had also gotten into the car. The guy leaned back into the car seat and chuckled.

"I'm fine" he said his lips curling upwards.

"Those bastards" He muttered quietly while Black started the car.

"What hostel do you stay?" Black asked turning to Jemima.

"I stay at Queen Roseline Hall of Residence" Jemima replied turning to take another glance at the guy seating at the back.

None of the trio said a word to each other till they reached Jemima's hostel. Jemima yawned grabbing her tote bag and pulled it over her shoulders before getting down from the car.

"Thank you Black" Jemima said.

"What's your real name?" Jemima asked.

"Abraham"

04 'FOUR'

J emima didn't bother going to her room instantly walking towards Doyin's room the moment she got to her floor. She knocked on the door and walked into the room giving Doyin's roommates polite smiles before crashing on Doyin's bed.

"I thought you and your brother went out?" Doyin said and Jemima nodded yawning.

"Yeah we did" Jemima replied pursing her lips.

"Almost turned me to a third party" she added and Doyin laughed pausing what she was doing to fall well.

"Third party?" She asked while Jemima nodded.

"En. Bimbo came over too" Jemima replied and Doyin nodded.

"I thought it was just a rumor that they were dating. You know your brother has a lot of fans and a lot of girls crushing on him" Doyin said while Jemima burst into laughter.

"It has been that way since we were little. Advantages of having fine ass parents" Jemima replied causing everyone in the room burst into laughter.

"Besides, my brother and Bimbo have a long history. You don't want to hear it though. And they've been dating since secondary school" Jemima added and Doyin nodded grateful for the inside information. No matter what the forums or rumors said, both Bimbo and Jeremiah had never bothered to explain to anyone so no one knew nothing in particular and could only make guesses.

"That's so nice" she said winking at Jemima.

"What about you?" She asked while Jemima chuckled.

"I'm hungry" she replied and Doyin burst into laughter holding her stomach while bending and breaking into fits of laughter.

"What part of whenever you are in trouble, send for help don't you understand Toni?" Black barked at Toni and the latter swallowed his saliva.

"I was surrounded Black. In that situation, do you think they would even allow me to use my phone?" Toni asked while Black hissed lightly flashing his pass at the security guard who saluted him as he sped out of the school.

Toni stretched his hand towards one of the buttons and pressed a button; the partition immediately moved and started closing while Black slammed on the accelerator. He sped through the busy student streets before turning into a slightly quiet street. Compared to other streets, the shops were well arranged and the owners weren't yelling or there wasn't half of the noise that came from other streets. Everyone who walked past the streets either walked quickly and chose to walk pass it at all.

Black slowly brought the car to a short stop in front of a house with a rather very high fence and horned twice. The gates was opened and he drove into the compound; parking the car with the horde of cars parked at the end at the garage.

The compound was filled with guys shirtless and hanging around doing all sorts of things; filling weights and people playing games, people just lounging without doing anything important. Black and Toni slapped handshakes with virtually everyone outside the house before they started walking towards the main house. Black pushed the door open to reveal some other guys playing PES in the seating room.

"My guyyy" Black called patiently slamming handshakes with the guys with a smile on his face..

"Toni, how far nah?" One of them asked.

"I dey o" Toni replied as Black walked towards the dinning table. There was a guy seating down on the dining table clad in a baggy skirt and the jeans that hugged his legs were ripped in different places, the low cut on his head wasn't too low but it certainly gave off a cool vibe. He heard footsteps and turned exposing a rather very feminine face and protruded chest.

"Queen, where's King?" Black asked while the girl raised her head and glanced at the duo.

"What is it?" She asked while Toni slipped his hands into his pockets swallowing his saliva for the thousandth time that afternoon.

"We need to talk to him" Toni replied and she chuckled.

"In his room" Queen replied returning back to what she was working on.

"He's in a bad mood" she added and both Black and Toni froze, wincing before they walked towards the hallway and walked down the hallway, stopping and knocking at the last door.

"Come in" someone said and they both stepped into the room.

Black sucked in a breadth turning the doorknob and pushing the door open to reveal a very spacious room. It was extremely neat clean and tidy with nothing looking out of place. A king sized bed stood up the left hand side hugging the wall while a poster of Kobe Bryant hung few meters above the bed frame. A reading table and chair with two laptops on it was seating at his right hand side with a rather huge shelf standing next to it.

A guy stood at the window with his back to them shirtless. Wisps of white smoke formed an halo around him making it unable to see his face. Despite the fact that they couldn't see his face, one could clearly see the way his back muscles contracted and straightened out as he breathed. It was obvious that this was somebody who worked out tirelessly.

His back muscles contracted again as he slowly turned to them while still holding a cigarette in between his fingers. He blew out white wisps of smoke and within minutes the wisps of smoke scattered showing a clearer picture of the guy who was standing. A rather very exquisite face came into view. The face looked like it was sculptured carefully with an artist because the high cheekbones and flat nose looked too perfect to be for a human. His lips were plump and looked as inviting as it could despite the fact that he had just stopped smoking. His charcoal eyes were attractive and deep and looked like they were capable of swallowing anyone who stared for too long.

Black had been seeing that face for three years good years yet he couldn't get over the tingles that spread across his body each time he met his gaze. He immediately lowered his head after meeting his eyes for a second.

"What happened?" He asked and Black swallowed his saliva.

"The Ravens" Black replied while the guy cocked an eyebrow at them.

"You don't mean it" he said his deep voice and his accent mixing together to form a rather kind of sexy and alluring tone.

"Right under my nose, The Ravens tried to injure one of my own?" He asked and Toni glanced at Black through the corner of his eyes.

"Actually King, there is something I haven't told you" Toni said while Black glanced at Toni with a hateful mixed with surprise glare.

"They got your sister" King replied and Toni raised his head shock and surprise boldly written all over his face.

"King" he called out quietly and the latter looked at him with disdain.

"Black, get me a shirt from that wardrobe" he said while Black glanced at Toni again before walking towards the inbuilt wardrobe and opened it; revealing a row of different shirts. He removed one of the shirts from the hanger and walked towards King, handling him the shirt.

"Toni, how long have you been with us?" King asked and Toni immediately fell to his knees bowing his head and shivering without replying.

King darted a glance at the shivering kneeling boy before walking out of the room, his legs long and his strides elegant.

"King" Black called out quietly as King continued walking.

"Let's go for a drive" he said as he stepped into the seating room. The guys playing PES immediately rushed to their feet as soon as King stepped into the seating room.

"King" they chorused and the latter merely waved at them walking out of the house. Queen dropped what she was doing and immediately hurried after him while Black walked towards a Toyota Camry, it was much less flashy and conspicuous compared to his sports car but the elegance and exquisiteness wasn't bad compared to it.

"Where are you going? I want to go" she said and King glanced at her without a word before getting into the car.

Black glanced at the duo as he winced "King" he called quietly.

"She's not going" King finally replied and Black glanced at her before getting into the driver's seat and ignited the engine. He reversed the car and drove out of the compound under everyone's watch.

"Where are we going King?" Black asked as soon as he drove into the main street.

"School" King replied bringing out his phone from his pockets and dialing a number and pressing the phone to his ears. The other person picked up the call on the second ring.

"King" he called in a respectful voice.

"Pay Allen a visit" King replied and Black glanced at King ; a huge smile forming on his lips.

"Yes King" the latter replied and King ended the call dropping the phone in one of the car's compartment before folding his arms. He pressed his chair backwards a bit leaning back into the chair.

"Go to Queen Amina Hall of Residence" King said and Black slammed on the accelerator as soon as he drove into the school compound.

"The rate of cultism is very high here in CUA" Doyin said and Jemima nodded her head eager to understand what Doyin was saying.

"I read a post on the school forum about this cult, Ravens or something like that" Jemima said and Paul nodded.

"They are one of the biggest cults in this school. You don't want to mess with them or get on their bad sides" Paul replied while Peter didn't say anything.

"How do we even know if people are cultists or not? I mean they don't write it on their forehead do they?" Jemima asked and they all burst into laughter.

"The last thing I wanna do is to get on the bad side of someone from Raven" Jemima added and Peter chuckled.

"Raven is one of the biggest but have you heard about the Titans?" Peter asked and Jemima furrowed her brows.

"I don't think so" Jemima replied crossing her legs.

"What about them? Are they as scary as The Ravens?" Jemima asked making Doyin chuckle.

"You really haven't heard about them?" Doyin asked and Jemima shook her head her negetively.

"No, I haven't" Jemima replied curiosity welling up in her.

"You are probably the only one in the whole of CUA that doesn't know about The Titans" Paul replied and Jemima immediately hitched closer to them.

"Are they really that popular? I read a lot of posts on the school forum, how come I've never even seen one of them?" Jemima asked.

"That's because everyone is scared of writing about them" Paul replied.

"Scared? They are more scarier than The Ravens?" Jemima asked and Peter nodded.

"Compared to the Titans, The Ravens isn't no big deal" Peter replied and Jemima's eyes widened.

"That scary?" Jemima whispered and Doyin nodded.

"I heard this story that a lecturer punished a student without knowing he was a member of The Titans. Apparently, the lecturer had been messing around with some female students. So he had set his eyes on this girl in his class and had been making subtle advances towards her but the girl had refused repeatedly. He always saw this guy and the girl together so he made it his duty to embarrass and punish the boy during his classes. He would fail him during tests and assignments and it was beginning to be obvious that he was intentionally picking on him" Doyin started as Jemima frowned.

"That's crazy. How would a lecturer treat a student like that. He isn't even sure if the boy and the girl are a thing. I hate people like this this most" she muttered as Doyin laughed.

"I haven't even gotten to the fun part" she said continuing her story.

"At first, the boy was taking all the harassment and embarrassment the lecturer made him go through because he was confused as to why the lecturer was picking on him. It wasn't until the lecturer almost molested his girlfriend in the office and was caught by some other students that he finally got a wind of what was going on and what his girlfriend had been hiding from him. As usual one day, he punished the guy during his class and tried to invite the girl to an hotel as leverage that he would stop harassing her boyfriend in the during class" Doyin added and Jemima immediately cut her short.

"What the hell? That's some crazy kind of blackmail. I thought lecturers like this only existed in public universities" Jemima said anger thoroughly brewing in her.

"That's so unfair to the boy and the girl" She added and Doyin laughed.

"You would let me finish bah?" she asked and Jemima laughed lightly.

"I'm sorry for cutting you short, continue the story" she replied adjusting her seating position to continue listening to Doyin.

"Barely two days later, some videos of him with some female students in a hotel got leaked" Doyin started and Jemima's eyes widened.

"Wow" Jemima muttered slowly.

"The videos went viral and was all over the forum. People wouldn't stop talking about it and a petition was immediately opened for the female students that had been harassed by him. The videos were also sent to the school management by different students in anger. The very next morning; he was found early in the morning in front of the Student Union building naked" Doyin added and Jemima burst into laughter.

"Wait, naked?" She asked in shock and Doyin nodded.

"Yes. Naked" Doyin replied and Jemima frowned still laughing.

"That's totally gross" She said and Doyin sighed.

"It was a big embarrassment for him when he woke up. The students had ganged up against him and took serval videos and pictures o f him naked. The school who apparently had bene ignoring him because I later heard he had a tight connection to the government or something couldn't ignore the issue and ended up sacking him," Doyin continued and Jemimah nodded her head.

"That's very good" Jemima said nodding her head.

"The students asked the school management to run a check on other lecturers who had the same issues and about four other lecturers were also sacked. Nobody said a word about it but both the school and the students knew who's doing it was. After that time, it was even harder to mess with them and the fear that only had roots in everyone's hearts grew and had branches" Doyin finished and Jemima folded her arms.

"As much as I want to applaud them for standing up for their own, that's some very scary shit. the fact they are students and they are able to pull it off is scarier sound very scary" Jemima muttered.

"That's if you get on their bad side. Some of the key members are well known in the school" Paul said and Jemima's eyes widened.

"You mean, you know some of them?" Jemima asked and Paul laughed.

"Not just me. Everyone knows some of them" Paul replied while Jemima rubbed her shoulders.

"I don't want to run into any of them in my stay in this school" Jemima muttered and the boys burst into laughter.

"You can't be so sure if you've ran into them or not" Peter murmured while Jemima glared at him.

"If you are one, you can start talking" Jemima said making Paul burst into laughter.

"Why? You'll stop being our friends if we are one?" Paul asked and Jemima shrugged her shoulders.

"Exactly" she replied as Paul sighed.

"Lucky us. We aren't" Paul said as Jemima sighed.

"What about other cults?" She asked.

"Every other cult in CUA is subject to The Titans. No one can mess with them even the school can't" Peter replied and Jemima folded her arms.

"The school can't? I don't get. You mean the school can't do anything when it comes to them?" Jemima asked surprised while Paul nodded.

"Exactly. Whenever matters that concerns The Titans occurs in the school, the school acts like they know nothing about it. The Titans have a huge network of connections than you think it is, it's not your usual kind of cult" Paul replied.

"Wow" she whispered.

"The very day we resumed, some cults got courage from God knows where and suddenly decided to attack a small group of The Titans, two students died and the rest landed in the hospital. The school didn't make a statement and even when someone reported to the Police, the school said the fight happened outside the school" Paul said and Jemima sucked in her breath at the shivers that coursed through her body in that moment while shaking her head.

"I want to have nothing to do with this murders" she muttered quietly.

05 | FIVE |

A loud yell cut Doyin's words and they all turned towards the door of the lecture theater where the yell came from.

"What happened?" Jemima asked, standing up to her feet like every other person. She glanced at her side to realize that Doyin was already at the door with other students craning their necks to see what was going on. She immediately hurried towards the entrance of the lecture room to see what was going on.

About four girls were at the center of the whole mess. One of the girls was on the floor, her leg slightly bruised with blood oozing quietly from the small cut while two other girls stood beside her facing another girl.

The girl has a baggy round neck that Jemima immediately realized was a limited edition round neck that was quite popular on Instagram. Sewa has told her she wanted to get one but it was already sold out.

The aphrodite jeans she wore cling to her lean and attractive legs and a lot of fancy chain sandals covered her feet but showed off her painted, well manicured toe nails. Her butterfly love was packed in a stylish bun accenting her round and beautiful face. Her face was caked in a frown while facing the three other girls.

"Did you have to push her?" One of the girls standing beside the injured girl asked glaring at the other girl hatefully.

"I told you that it was a reflex action and I did not know" the girl on the butterfly locs shot back.

"You did not know?" The other girl asked.

"She merely wanted to hold you for support and you pushed her" she added while the girl on butterfly locs chuckled.

"Hold me for support? She wanted to grab my clothes!" She yelled back.

"Isn't it the same thing? All in all she was preventing herself from falling"

"At the expense of my clothes?"

J

"Clothes? Annabelle, can you hear yourself? You would rather get someone injured than allow a stain on your shirt?"

"How much is the round neck anyways?" The other girl shot at her.

"Just the round neck would buy the entirety of what you are wearing, The three of you, my round neck would buy everything you are wearing, the shirts, the blouses, the sandals and slippers and your 15k wig included" Annabelle replied while some of the students burst into laughter.

"Do you have to insult us like that? I was the one who wanted to hold your clothes for support. Must you ridicule my friends?" the injured girl asked and Annabelle shrugged.

"Of course. You are letting them be your Super Girl, anything that comes with trying to reason with you grabbing my shirt; they should take it with their arms wide open" Annabelle replied and the girl pursed her lips.

"You know y'all have a way of making someone out to be a horrible person. Y'all were gossiping about someone else and you didn't look at where you were going; then you tried to grab my own clothes to support yourself?" Annabelle asked.

"Girl I was merely walking in front of you and you couldn't grab your friends' clothes except mine. And you do realize that grabbing my shirt would have pulled me down with you right?" Annabelle asked again as another girl interrupted them.

"No matter guy Anna; you shouldn't have pushed her. She's bleeding"

"She was going to fall anyways; how is that my fault?" Annabelle asked.

"Guy!"

"I hate people touching me the most " Annabelle spat before glaring at the three girls and pushing her way through the crowd of students who immediately started making way for her to get through.

"She's too proud for my liking"

"Just because she's a model; she thinks she can walk over anyone as she likes"

"She's selfish"

"Can you imagine? She said her roundneck alone would buy the three of them clothes and hair!"

"How is that possible?"

"It is. I heard the round neck is limited edition"

"Must she show off at every opportunity she gets?"

"I don't like her one bit!"

The students who were already dispersing continued gossiping while Jemima folded her arms and turned to Paul who was standing beside her.

"Who's she?" She asked.

"Annabelle?"

"Yes"

"You don't know Annabelle?" Peter asked with a raised eyebrow.

"Her face looks familiar for some reason but I can't pinpoint where I might have seen her before"

"She's a model under SOLO" Paul said and Jemima turned to him in surprise.

"SOLO?" She asked in shock and Paul nodded her head.

"You know that shoot with Jamal? She was the one seated beside his leg" Paul replied and Jemima nodded her head.

"Oh yeah. She was the one" Jemima replied.

"She's also the spokesperson for BINTA right?" Jemima asked and Peter nodded her head.

"Yup"

"To think she's a student here" Jemima murmured.

"I'm sure it took you this long to recognize her. She's quite very popular in school" Peter said and Jemima turned to him.

"For being nasty?" She asked while Peter burst into laughter.

"I think that's written all over her forehead," Peter replied.

"I actually saw a post of another model at SOLO subtly hinting on how Annabelle badly treated the other models," Jemima said, folding her arms.

"Well, I did hear that she had her roommates moved to another room because they were too annoying. Then she paid for the whole room" Peter said.

"She lives in a school hostel?" Jemima asked in surprise.

"And in your own hostel" Paul replied.

"That's all levels of nasty. If she couldn't cope with having roommates, then nothing was stopping her from moving out of the hostel or paying for another room in the hostel. Did she have to have them moved to another room and embarrassed them?" Jemima asked, sitting back on her seat, a frown marring her face.

"I don't think Annabelle cares about all that though" Paul replies, scrolling through his phone.

"This blogger has made a post again" he muttered;

"What post?" Jemima asked.

"Open the school forum"

Jemima grabbed her phone from her back pocket and scrolled it open. She was quick to open the school forum and indeed, someone had made a post of what had just happened. A clear shot of where Annabelle was glaring at the three girls was the headshot.

BULLYING: MY CLOTHES WOULD BUY YOURS

A deeper frown appeared on Jemima's face upon reading the title.

"What kind of title is this? Who posted this?" Jemima asked.

"No one knows who he or she is. It's a new blogger on the forum but somehow drops juicy contents" Paul replied scrolling through the post.

"Bullying? We clearly saw what happened. Annabelle was indeed at fault for pushing the girl but the girl indeed pulled her first" Jemima replied scrolling through the post as well.

"This person is such a crook; what's this post?" Jemima asked angrily.

"Just calm down. Don't take it to heart" Peter said consoling Jemima who suddenly looked around in confusion.

"Where's Doyin?" She asked.

"She wanted to use the restroom so she left while we were watching what happened" Paul replied.

"Okay" Jemima replied, proceeding to open the blogger's page and scroll through the previous posts.

"Butter Fairy?" Jemima asked no one in particular before chuckling and closeting the page.

"I don't know why people choose to be so poisonous" she added and Peter laughed again.

"It's not that deep, Jemima. Someone would think you are defending Annabelle" Peter replied and Jemima turned to him.

"Not that deep? Of course it's not that deep to you basically because you are not the one who has been talked about and over three thousand people are reading. You clearly saw what happened and you know what this blog post says and what happened are two different things" Jemima started.

"Annabelle might be nasty and whatnot but I don't think it's right to paint her a villain when clearly both ladies were at fault in this issue" Jemima finished and sighed.

"I don't know why I'm getting worked up too. I don't like her" she muttered while Paul and Peter burst into laughter.

"Annabelle is lucky sort of lucky; having random strangers speak up for her"

06 ' SIX '

Annabelle scrolled through her phone; grim lines spreading across her face. Reading the blog post made her cackle into laughter. This was someone she doubted even knew her and probably heard the story from a third party yet claimed that she bullied them.

Annabelle could never understand humans; they way their thought process happened and what went on in their heads. Sometimes she badly wanted to crack some of some skulls open and check whether they actually had pear sized brains or it was just a compilation of nerve endings.

A call came inhaling her eyes off the headline of the blog post. She scrolled the accept call button while placing the phone on the table and putting it on a loudspeaker.

"Annabelle, I heard something happened in school" an exasperated voice came through the phone and Annabelle immediately snickered.

"You heard already? News sure does travel fast" Annabelle replied folding her arms and shaking her head.

"What do you mean I heard already? Have you forgotten what Director Ajose said to you?" The voice asked again even more exasperated than when she first spoke. Annabelle's smile was immediately wiped off by her statement and she sighed again, rubbing her forehead.

"It was not my fault okay? They were gossiping and she tried to pull on my..." Annabelle started replying and paused half way in her statement.

"Oh I forgot; I bullied them, that's what happened" she finished pursing her lips.

"Annabelle! Why would you bully someone else? If the news gets out; how are your fans going to defend you?!"

"Fans? If you want to pull a card; pull a card that actually exists okay?" Annabelle shot at her a frown marring her face.

"Just stay under the radar Annabelle. One more strike and you are out. So please Anna, please"

Annabelle glanced at her phone and ended the call.

They were all the same. Humans.

Annabelle was yet to stand up from her seat when two girls approached her nervously. Her eyebrow wriggled uprightly seeing them and her eyes twinkled intentionally asking them what they wanted with her eyes.

"Hi Annabelle, my name is Sarah"

"Hi Sarah, nice to meet you. How may I help you?" Anabbelle asked, folding her arms. Sarah played with her fingers nervously as her friend tugged on her shirt urging to speak up. Realizing that Sarah was too nervous to say anything; Annabelle turned to her friend.

"Why don't you tell me what she's doing in front of me?" Annabelle asked and her friend frowned slightly at Annabelle's tone.

"She's auditioning to be a model at SOLO, so she thinks if you take a few pictures with her; it could increase her chances of being picked," her friend replied and Annabelle burst into laughter.

"You won't get picked," she replied with a straight face that froze both girls.

"Excuse me?" Sarah stuttered out.

"I said you won't get picked," Annabelle replied, still wearing a straight face.

"Annabelle!" her friend exclaimed.

"That's so rude! Must you be nasty and overbearing every time?" she asked, glaring hatefully at Annabelle who merely chuckled at their change in expressions.

"Aren't you supposed to ask me why?" she asked and both girls decided to keep mute watching as a small smile spread across her lips.

"I'll tell you why you came to me" Annabelle started watching every single expression that crossed their faces.

"You went for the physical interview and you flopped. Of course your stuttering is already a major turn off, I'm sure Director Banks started frowning the moment you opened your mouth" Annabelle revealed and Sarah stared at her with wide eyes.

"You... You... You...." Sarah stuttered, unable to get a word out of her mouth.

"You realized that you had failed even if no one told you you had. You saw the expression on their faces. Human actions of course speak louder than their words" Annabelle added, shaking her head as she continued.

"So you thought of something that could give you a leeway compared to others. Something the board might have to consider. And that was taking pictures with a top model of SOLO and feigning familiarity"

The look of shock and surprise by now was fully evident on both Sarah's and her friend's face. They both stared at Annabelle in horror but the latter wasn't done speaking.

"But where are you going to run into a top model of SOLO? Where are you going to run into Jamal or Drew? Where are you going to find Prisca or Ruth? I mean they don't even live in Akure. They are at the headquarters, not only did you have access to meet them, you had zero chances of taking a picture with them even if you did" Annabelle continued relaxing back into her seat as she raised her head to meet both of their eyes.

"Then it crossed your mind; there's one in your school but she's so nasty and overbearing! How do you do it? You had to do it, even if i embarrassed you or insulted you it was fine as long as i agreed to take a picture with you or better still if someone took a video of us talking and posted it online like your friend outside is doing. I bet if she can hear; the phone would have dropped and that would be her saying bye byes to her lovely phone"

"That's why you are in front of me Sarah. To get a picture and feign familiarity. You are not hoping that the picture gives you a chance, you are hoping that when they see the picture; they will be forced to give you a chance" Annabelle announced, chuckling.

"You are funny though. Very funny. A model who wants to join SOLO but you do not know the basic core values that SOLO works with. You have zero idea of how the system works. You have not looked closely at those top SOLO models you want to be like so much and maybe imagined being friends with them when you get in. You didn't look at them and find what was common even though everyone is different"

"You for sure have a smart and poisonous mind; that's if all these were cooked up by you though but you lack not just the aura but the confidence. And that's exactly what SOLO wants in their models. Confidence; a stuttering person like you can never be a model or if a model, under SOLO. That was why I told you; you wouldn't get picked." Annabelle finished sighing softly.

"I'm amazed at how bold you are, Sarah. You actually had the guts to try to use me? Who gave you the boldness? How dare you?" Annabelle asked with a smile on her lips.

"I am nasty and overbearing and whatever names you call me behind my back. I know, I know very well that none of you is bold enough to walk up to me and call me those names to my face because whether I am overbearing or not, you still have to look at me with respect because of where I am. And you, you stammerer dared to use me" Annabelle continued chuckling lightly while clapping her hands.

She rose to her feet while grabbing the tote bag on the table. Sarah and her friend instinctively jumped back and Annabelle burst into laughter.

"Wait, did you think I was going to hit you? Why would I do that?" Annabelle asked before smiling again.

"I can pick up my phone right now and put a call across to the board or recruiting Directors. A contestant tried to use foul means to force them to give her another chance. You know if you really wanted to be a model at SOLO despite your stutters; you would know what to do and how to win the favor of those Directors. I can assure you that they aren't that hard to please " Annabelle stated shrugging her shoulders.

"If you actually made the effort to do any research about SOLO, you'll find out that dishonest people are people they despise the most. People like you. And guess what happens if I put a call across to them?" Annabelle asked with another smile. She could see Sarah already shaking and holding onto her friend for support.

"Not only will you be disqualified; you will also never in your entire existence have a chance to audition at SOLO again" Annabelle revealed and Sarah staggered backwards.

"You do not want to be a model at SOLO Sarah, what you want and like is the fame and luxury that comes with being a model there and what you do not know is that, we work hard. Very hard. You only see the beautiful side, the side where we work hard and struggle to bring out just the best of us; you don't see it. You think being a model is all about the likes, the comments and the popularity?" Annabelle asked.

"Leemaoo" she muttered laughing as she started walking away.

"Be very grateful i refused to take a picture with you today else you would have certainly gotten banned" Annabelle added pausing in her steps and turning towards the girls.

"Tell your friend to also delete the video. I'm sure she needs to delete some other things to keep the video, she might as well delete it" she said looking towards the door where a small phone camera was showing slightly. Chuckling lightly, she resumed her journey and continued walking away shaking her head.

Human, humans, humans; she never understood how their thought process worked.

I don't know if your opinion of Annabelle has changed with this chapter but mine hasn't really changed. She's nuts.... it's the 'Leemaoo' part for me.

I finished this up at some minutes to 2 in the morning so I couldn't laugh out well but it was hell as funny.

And I'm also sure some of you would have roasted Sarah by now. Like premium dragging but I also want you to ask yourself, are you not like Sarah? The issue here is not being a model, are you not going through hell and water for something you barley know about just because you like the situations and the luxury that comes with it? I don't know why I'm sounding like a sage all of a sudden but honestly yeah, remember to check yourself.

Hehehe, I'm working very hard to keep to my actually promise of two chapters per week and for this week; this is the second chapter. Thank you very much for the 1K reads people. I'll be going to camp next week so there's a chance that only one chapter might be uploaded but I'll try as much as possible to make it long and juicy.

With so much love to you alllllllllll.

07 'SEVEN'

F or some very weird reason, Jemima, Doyin, Paul and Peter soon became a very popular squad in their Faculties and Departments. And although Jemima didn't care if she got more or less attention; she had somehow always managed to get or attract attention wherever she found herself. Whether it was less or more didn't make a difference.

Although only Jemima and Paul were in the same department and Faculty; Peter and Doyin who were also in different departments and faculties always found a way to hang out with them. Jemima's Instagram page which always had very familiar faces was greeted with new unfamiliar faces twice. Faces of Doyin, Paul and Peter.

"Why do we already offer departmental courses that's 4-unit in 100 level and you guys just get to offer general courses huh?" Jemima asked no one in particular, slamming her books shut in slight annoyance. It was enough that the course was a 4-unit course but the lecturer was extremely un-understandable so they had to do research on their own and reach out to the students in higher levels. Jemima, who had a hard time communicating with other people, found it hard to reach out to the students in higher levels.

It then fell to the shoulders of Paul who wasn't much of a social butterfly as well to find some of the students in the higher levels and after a while managed to get some PDFs and a few handouts. It wasn't then that they both realized that the course was much harder than they thought. They were the ones who chose Medicine and Surgery, no one asked them to so whatever madness their faculty and department came up with, they had to chest it. Those were Paul's words, by the way.

"Why are you wearing such a murderous face?" Doyin asked, climbing up the steps and stopping in front of the Jemima and the boys.

"She's complaining about BCH101" Paul replied, yawning while Doyin rolled her eyes.

"I hate that course. That is why I didn't go to science class in the first place" she muttered through her teeth and Peter burst into laughter.

"So what did the red-haired girl want to do with you?" Jemima asked and Doyin wore a face.

"You don't know Heraline xoxo as well?" Doyin asked and Jemima shook her head.

"I'm sure I've heard that name somewhere but it's not clicking right now" Jemima replied, running her hands through her hair.

"Heraline xoxo is that girl that draws and has this sort of gothic style" Doyin revealed reluctantly while Jemima's eyebrows shot up in remembrance.

"I remember her. She also has this street kind of style" Jemimah added and Doyin nodded her head.

"So what did she want with you?" Jemima asked bringing Doyin back to the reason why they were speaking about her in the first place.

"She gave you invitation cards to her party?" Peter asked seeing the red cards in Doyin's hands. The latter turned to him with a glare.

"Don't ruin my surprise" she spat at him while Peter threw his hands up laughing.

"So Heraline wanted me to have an invitation card to the party she's throwing this weekend. I figured out that we needed to go since you need a distraction from these " Doyin said pointing disdainfully at the books in front of Jemima.

"So you in?" Doyin asked gleefully and Jemima nodded her head.

"Sure. I haven't been to a party since I resumed" she replied, packing up the books into her bag.

"So here's the crazier thing if we want to go for this party" Doyin started and Paul yawned again.

"You have to dress in gothic or street style?" he asked and Doyin turned to him, sending him a punch to his shoulder.

"I said, do not ruin my surprise!" she yelled and the rest burst into laughter.

"That's a given considering the parties she had thrown in the past. I have seen a few of the pictures" Jemima replied while Doyin folded her hands sulking.

"So are you going to go with the street style?" Jemima asked and Doyin pursed her lips.

"I've never tried the gothic style before because I am unsure of how it would look on me although i want to try it badly" Doyin replied and Jemima nodded her head.

"So are you trying it or not?" she asked and Doyin shook her head.

"If I want to explore the styles that would look good on me, I'm not doing that at Heraline's party," Doyin replied while Jemima burst into laughter.

"Are you guys coming too?" Jemima asked, turning to the boys. Instead of replying to her, Paul immediately stretched his hand out to relieve her of the weight of her tote bag.

"Paul and Peter do not like parties. They didn't even come to the bowling night" Doyin replied and Jemima stared at both of them in surprise.

"PTSD" Paul replied with a grin while Peter merely nodded his head without saying anything else. Jemima was quick to catch up on the fact that it was a topic they weren't interested in discussing.

"Send us all the pictures you take by the way," Peter added, grinning.

"Doyin, do not try the gothic style by the way. I have a bad feeling about it" he continued causing everyone to laugh and Doyin throw him another punch to his stomach.

"Yup: now I envy Heraline though. Her gothic style is so chic" Doyin muttered rubbing her chin.

"Do you know how long she had to try those styles indoors before she came to the internet with them?" Jemima asked and Doyin turned to her.

"She tried them indoors?" she asked in sheer surprise.

"I saw an interview where she said she dyed her hair in different colours and saw how they looked on her before choosing the ones who looked good on her before coming out with them, " Jemima replied.

"But red looks so good on her. She isn't even fair complexioned" Doyin grumbled and Peter laughed again.

"You don't even have outfits to go in gothic style so what's this sweat and grumbling for?" Peter asked and Doyin folded her arms again.

"Just shut up" Doyin muttered and Paul raised his phone.

"The party is sure going to be crowded. Butterfly Fairy already made a post" Paul announced and Jemima rolled her eyes.

"That girl sure is a big gossip" Jemima muttered.

"Why are you concluding that it's a girl?" Paul asked and Jemima shrugged her shoulders.

"Instincts or something like that" She replied and Doyin chuckled.

"She already has over seven hundred followers by the way," Doyin added, turning to Jemima who also brought out her phone to search through the school forum.

The school forum was like a mini Instagram website. You could post pictures, run polls, post whatever and ask questions. Some of the students had turned their accounts to a blog posting information and gossip on their accts turning them to the most followed accounts on the school forum and somehow ButterFly Fairy whose account was new already had over seven hundred followers competing with some of the old bloggers.

It was obvious the latter wasn't a new student because she somehow knew the trends and things happening in school. Before any of the other bloggers got wind of some news, she would have posted it and would have even gotten traction so by the time the others saw the news and ran to the forum to post it they would realize that it would already be a trending topic.

"Whoever is sure has guts. I heard that Janet is looking for her" Doyin said, shaking her head.

Janet was one or rather used to be the one with all the news, she always had first hand giving her lots of popularity and had one of the highest following on the school forum with over ten thousand followers but Butterfly Fairy was already giving her some kind of serious problems that was already causing rumours to fly around. Another rumour was flying around that Janet had asked that if anyone knew who ButterFly Fairy was, such a person should come to her.

"She's just been overbearing. If ButterFly Fairy gets all the gists before her; it's her fault that she's so slow. What did she mean by finding ButterFly Fairy? Would she beat her up? I hope she's someone who had a cultist as her boyfriend" Jemima muttered and Doyin bent over her stomach in laughter.

"God Jemima" Doyin muttered through her laughter.

"I thought you didn't like Butterfly Fairy, " Paul said.

"Well I don't like her. She's too nosy and likes to paint other people in bad light" Jemima replied shrugging her shoulders.

"Why are you on her side now?" Peter asked, folding his arms.

"Something about your guts again?" he asked again and Jemima pursed her lips.

"I don't think so," she replied.

"You were like this when that issue with Annabelle happened the last time" Paul pointed out and Jemima sighed.

"We were all there so we know exactly what went down but just look at how ButterFly Fairy wrote what happened" Jemima said, folding her arms.

"Why are we talking about Annabelle and ButterFly Fairy when we have a party to go to?" Jemima asked.

"The party is not until tomorrow night Jemmy" Doin said as they started walking towards their hostel.

"You already have something to wear in your head?" Paul asked, slipping his hands into his pockets and falling into steps with Jemima who nodded her head.

"Farida wore this outfit to this street party, so I have an idea on what to wear," Jemima replied, nodding her head.

Hello guysssss; I missed you all. First I want to apologize for the delay in the updates. Camp was really stressful and I ended up taking a very long time to rest. So for this week, expect another update by Friday or Saturday. I'm cooking for you guysssss.

Meanwhile, if anyone of you voted for me to be interviewed in my recent interview, I want to say a big thank you to you. I know I'm not as consistent as before but yet you guys always show up for me; for that I want to say another thank you. I enjoyed the session by the way.

This chapter is vibes on vibes, I've dropped some many side plots and themes in this chapter and if you people don't catch it; you'll end up catching it in the other chapters so make I no yarn anything.

Who's excited for the party? Guess the people that are meeting???? I owe you money if you guess right.

Meanwhile don't forget to spam with votes and likes. I love you guys.

08 | EIGHT

Jemima and Doyin soon realized that the Heraline xoxo party wasn't a small party and a lot of people were invited. She was just in her second year but her influence in the school was quite huge. It was normal given that she was an Instagram influencer. To get into the party; you needed an invitation card and how Doyin and Jemima got one; both of them had no idea.

"I just can't seem to think of any connection between us" Doyin muttered, adjusting her head that was on Peter's lap.

"Are you sure you've not run into her at school or something?" Peter asked and Doyin shook her head.

"I don't think so. She's in the Faculty of Engineering; our paths will almost not cross and have in actuality never crossed. I have no idea of why she would have specially come to look for me to give me an invitation card" Doyin replied.

"Do you think someone asked her to give it to you?" Peter asked and Doyin shook her head.

"I may be a social butterfly but I don't think I know anyone that could ask Heraline to give me an invitation card to her party"

"Infact; the 100 level students attending her party are not even that much. I heard that only five students in Engineering got the invitation" Paul added and Doyin cocked her head.

"Please go to the party and ask her then" Jemima concluded.

"Do you know where the party is?" Paul asked.

"Yes. I asked around and it's a popular hotel near the school gate" Doyin replied nodding her head while Paul shrugged his shoulders.

"If you know where it is that's fine too" Paul muttered.

"Don't worry yourself too much, we are not babies and we can certainly take care of ourselves" Doyin said and Paul nodded his head turning to meet Peter's amused eyes.

Jemima could feel her roommates boring holes into her head and her body. Doyin had made sure she was loud enough when talking to her roommates that she was one of the few that got invited to Heraline's party. In fact, there were already rumours flying around of how Heraline herself had come to personally give Doyin the invitation card.

"Does she know Heraline?" She could hear Tamiloore whispering to Vickie who had her arms folded and was boring hole into her head.

For someone like Vickie who prided herself as classy and sophisticated, not getting an invitation to Heraline's party was a slap on her face.

"Is it true that Heraline xoxo came to give them the invitation card themselves?" Ayisat whispered, watching as Jemima sat on her bed tying her shoelaces.

The street style Farida had worn for a street festival had somehow gone viral on the internet. She was a princess and was an unrestrained one at that. Jemima had planned to wear something similar but at the end of the day chose to go with crazy baggy jeans and a crop top. After tying her laces, she rose to her feet and walked towards the wardrobe opening her jewelry box and fixing her magnetic belly button.

Jemima had no reason to why she was dressing up so much in the first place, she just wanted to look good, maybe really good because she knew no one, absolutely no one would under-dress to Heraline's party. She looked at the mirror in front of her while carefully applying her lip gloss.

"God, she looks good" Ayisat said aloud while Vickie turned to glare at her.

The door was immediately opened and Doyin walked into the room, her eyes bulging widely while staring at Jemima who slipped her hands into her pockets and raised her head up slightly.

"How do I look?" she asked.

"Sexy. You look so good and.... Oh my god! You have a belly piercing?" Doyin shouted and Jemima burst into laughter.

"My mom would kill me, it's magnetic" Jemima replied and Doyin covered her mouth staring at Jemima again.

"I'm straight, I'm straight in the name of Jesus" Doyin muttered while Jemima shook her head at her still laughing. She was clad in a black round neck with XOXO boldly written on it and very small shorts that barely covered her thighs. The round neck and the shorts were about the same length. She went ahead to wear a net stockings to cover her thighs and her legs using boots as her footwear. She ended up wearing a slight gothic style.

"Could you please take our picture?" Doyin asked grinning as she stretched her phone towards Vickie who stared at both Doyin and the phone before collecting it from her.

"Thank you" Doyin grinned again, grabbing Jemima and posing with her. Vickie took a few shots and Jemima carried her bag.

"Let's go" she said and they both stepped out of the room while many eyes followed them out of the hostel.

"Why do I have an inkling that Vickie must have made us very ugly when she took those pictures?" Doyin asked as they both walked out of the hostel getting into the Uber they had ordered before.

She opened her phone and scrolled through the pictures, a surprised expression spreading across her face.

"These are Instagram worthy pictures Jemi, Vickie could pass for a photographer" Doyin said passing the phone to Jemima to show her the pictures. And in reality; Doyin wasn't lying, Vickie had indeed taken the pictures well, all the angles, their smiles and giggles, their arrogance radiated off the pictures.

"I'm posting them to my story first, " Doyin said, scrolling through the pictures with glee.

"Remember to airdrop pictures mama" Jemima said smiling and scrolling through her phone. A notification appeared at the top of the screen. It was a message asking her if they had left the hostel yet. She quickly tapped on the message and replied to him telling him they had just left.

She vividly remembered when they had first met, their interactions and how she almost gave them away. The thoughts made her laugh and Doyin turned to her confused.

"Why are you laughing?" Doyin asked.

"Well, I just randomly remembered when we first met," Jemima replied and they both burst into laughter.

"Well, I'm glad I ran after you that day" Doyin replied and Jemima nodded her head.

"I'm glad too," she replied, her smile bigger.

Jemima and Doyin had apparently underestimated the influence of Her-aline in CUA, the hotel for the party was crowded with students and cars and loud music,

"Is that a fucking power bike?" Doyin asked her eyes wide and Jemima nodded her head at the loss of words.

"Yes Doyin. That's a mother fucking power bike" She whisper yelled. The bouncers at the entrance looked like they could snap heads in half if anyone messed with them and Doyin managed to wear a smile as they approached them. She stretched the card to them and one of them collected it from her scanning the card and the girls standing in front of them and returned the card to them.

"Can we go in now?" Doyin asked apprehensively. The one who had col-lected the card from them nodded his head and Doyin grabbed Jemima's hand while the both of them fled inside the party.

"God of mercy, how do they look like that?" Doyin asked and Jemima laughed looking around.

"This is almost like a fashion show" Doyin whispered while Jemima nod-ded her head taking notes of the styles and dresses.

"So what do we do now?" Doyin asked.

"Let's find a corner to sit in first. We'll look for Heraline later" Jemima replied and they both tried to paraphrase their way through the numerous students to another corner of the party. Several people were moving around carrying cocktails and drinks; Jemima stopped one of them taking a drink off the tray and Doyin also stretched and took one too. She then offered the server a smile.

"Thank you".

"Do you have an idea of what we carried?" Doyin asked, sniffing the drink they had carried off the tray.

"It's Sprite and lime" the server replied and Doyin turned to him.

"Ha" Doyin replied, chuckling.

"Do you have any idea where the bar is?" Doyin asked and the server nodded.

"What do you want me to bring for you?" Doyin asked and Jemima shook her head.

"I'm fine," She replied.

"Please lead the way," Doyin said to the server, who darted another glance at Jemima before lowering his tray and leading the way for Doyin.

Jemima scrolled through her phone replying to some of the texts and rolling her eyes at the fact that someone had mentioned that she was at Heraline xoxo's party. She sipped her drink squeezing her face at the taste. It was more of Lime with a sprinkle of sprite.

"You came" someone said above her head and looked upwards to meet Heraline eyes. The latter was obviously on contacts because grey eyes stared back at her and underneath the multicolored lights, Jemima had to admit that grey was a very beautiful colour of eyes.

"Did you think we wouldn't show up?" Jemimah asked, dropping the drink on the table.

"I wasn't sure" Heraline replied smiling and glancing at the drink Jemima had dropped on the table.

"It's bitter" Jemima replied and Heraline burst into laughter.

"Follow me, I'll give you a better one" Heraline replied, stretching her hand out and grabbing Jemima's hands much to her surprise.

"Heraline" Jemima called and Heraline turned to her. It was then that Jemima realized that she was dressed almost the same as Doyin except that she was wearing a very short skirt and a crop top instead.

"Huh?"

"Do you know me?" Jemima asked and Heraline grinned.

"Not really" she replied.

"Why did you give us an invitation card?" Jemima asked.

"Did someone ask you to?" Jemima asked again while Heraline furrowed her brows.

"Why would you think that?" Heraline asked.

"I saw your picture on FOMES and you were really pretty," Heraline replied."

"But it was Doyin who you gave the invitation card to," Jemima pointed out.

"She was outside when I came to find you so I just gave her and told her the card was for you" Heraline replied and Jemima nodded before raising her brows.

"Are you straight?" Jemima suddenly asked freezing Heraline in her steps. The latter turned to Jemima and then burst into laughter holding her stomach as she laughed.

"Girl what goes on in that head of yours?" She asked while Jemima purses her lips embarrassed.

"I'm sorry" she muttered quietly and Heraline nodded her head.

"You obviously aren't very informed about a lot of things in school are you? If you were, you would know I have a boyfriend" Heraline revealed and Jemima was further embarrassed.

"That's a very sexy belly piercing" She added and Jemima glanced at her stomach before smiling lightly.

"Thank you"

"Just follow me; let me introduce you to a few people," Heraline said and Jemima chuckled, allowing Heraline to pull her through the crowd. She was starting to realize the faces and eyes that were turning towards them as they walked past.

Heraline pulling around someone was rare and so everyone was curious of who she was pulling around.

"I thought you were going to get me a better drink," Jemima pointed out.

"There are better ones upstairs," she replied.

"Let me call Doyin. She went to get drinks" Jemima muttered digging into the pocket of her jeans to bring out her phone.

"I'll have someone bring her up later. Don't worry about her"

"Heraline" Jemima called for the second time that night.

"Huh?"

"What's your real name?" Jemima asked, suddenly realizing that she had never heard anyone address her as anything apart from Heraline or Heraline xoxo.

Heraline turned to her wearing a bright smile "Why are you curious?" She asked.

"Nothing. I think knowing that would make me feel closer to you or something" Jemima replied, pursing her lips.

"Badmus Waliyat Olajumoke; that's my name"

Yo peopleeeeeeeeeee I know you guys missed me and guys what? I missed you guys too. I'm trying to keep up with my promised of updating two chapters twice in a week but my laptop fucked up and there was really nothing I could do anything about it. I'm trying to fix it up and make adjustments so expect updates next week.

I'm yet to reply the last chapter comments but I know that you people were airing me. You people should go back and comment o, It won't be nice if the book gets hot and you start asking me, 'who's this' , 'when did this happen' me sef sabi air people.

You guys should take a guess, why and how did Doyin and Jemima get invited to Heraline's party? It's pretty easy if you read these two chapters well though and yes Heraline xoxo was inspired by no other person than . She's not like the Heraline xoxo in HYT but she does definitely gives off that kind of vibe.

And finally; the party is getting started. I'm getting really excited to write these scenes because hey are so funny and who are the peeps that are finally meetingggggggggg. I'm excited on their behalf please be excited on their behalf too, that's if you know who and who is meeting sha.

So guys, keep your fingers crossed and get ready for the spicy and hot hot hot stuffs I'm bringing. For those who asked about my writing IG account, I'm really sorry for not posting as I used to so I would be posting soon. A small game for you to play so just stay tuned till then.

I love youuuuuu.

09 'NINE'

Jemima had always been aware that CUA had a huge student population that she had never seen so many students clustered together in one place. Heraline led her through a passage and Jemima realized that it was another part of the club where another party was going on.

The music was sombre and one look at the people walking to and fro carrying cups of whatsoever, Jemima needed no one to tell her that it was Heraline's personal people.

Heads were already turning at their arrival and Jemima for once wanted to turn and walk away. The eyes were scrutinizing and questioning. But instead; Jemima walked with a straight face, refusing to show her discomfort.

Everyone wore their curiosity on their faces as they walked past them until Heraline stopped at a pool table that Jemimah hadn't noticed before. The boys or rather men at the table all stopped playing and turned to them both. Jemimah couldn't recognize some of the faces but she remembered seeing some of them on Instagram. It was then it became obvious to her that it wasn't just CUA students that were at the party and some people had come from their schools to attend Heraline's party.

"Heraline, who's this?" one of the boys asked with an amused smile and Heraline glared at him playfully.

"First, you take your eyes off my girl, she isn't available" Heraline replied.

"Well guys, This is Jemimah, an MBBS 100 level student.." Heraline didn't get to finish her statement when one of the boys interrupted her.

"I didn't want to say before but she definitely looks like someone who had A's on her WAEC" at his statement, the boys burst into laughter and Jemima chuckled pausing their laughter midway and getting their attention fully back on her.

"The more hilarious part is that I did have straight A's on my WAEC" Jemima replied a small smile on her face.

"But feel free to think I did it at some miracle centre or something like that" she added and the boy who had spoken before chuckled.

"What do you mean?" he asked.

"You look at me and you think, oh she can't be smart" Jemima replied while Heraline raised her eyebrow smiling with her eyes.

"I certainly wasn't thinking that" the guy replied and Jemima nodded her head.

"I believe you but everyone's faces is saying, nigga you lying" Jemima replied and everyone burst into laughter again.

"I like you," the guy said, nodding his head.

"Well I don't" Jemima shot back at him.

"Nice to meet you Jemima" another guy said, still laughing while stretching out his hand.

"I'm sure you like me too, " he added with a wink. Jemima chuckled lightly, taking his outstretched hand.

"Not really," She replied.

"I'm Muyiwa, nice to meet you"

And the next thirty minutes involved Heraline introducing Jemima to everyone else. Jemima wasn't so much a fan of meeting new people but the Heraline was introducing her to her big faces on Instagram and the cream of the creamiest top of the students of CUA.

Someone could basically say that Heraline was helping her build a network and why? Jemima had no idea but she is more than ready to integrate herself into the network.

Heraline snorted, pushing away the cup of alcohol someone had stretched to Jemima for the sixth time.

"I just said nobody offers her alcohol unless she asks for it" she said with a small frown and the girl who had offered Jemima the cup immediately raised her hands in reply.

"I didn't hear that" she muttered.

"Well now you have," Heraline added, pulling Jemima away.

"I'm so sorry about that. You shouldn't take alcohol if you are alone" Heraline added with a subtle wink while Jemima nodded her head.

"I understand," she replied.

"What do you want? Mocktails or just juice?" Heraline asked.

"I'd like to try the mocktails" she replied and someone walked towards Heraline flashing a grin at Jemima and she returned it quietly with a smile.

"King is here" the other person muttered and Heraline nodded her head.

"Jemima, let Ay take you to the bar so you can have your mocktail, I have to see someone" Heraline muttered and Jemima nodded.

"Okay" she muttered watching as Heraline walked away. Jemima turned to the guy who had come to inform her that someone was around and offered him a small smile.

"So you are Jemima" the boy started while he led the way towards the bar.

"You know me?" Jemima asked and Ay shook his head.

"I don't" he replied, pausing in his steps and turning to Jemima.

"Heraline has been holding your hands and dragging you through the party since you walked in, of course rumours are already flying around" Ay added and Jemima nodded her head unfazed.

"Rumors like what?" she asked.

"Just take a lot at the school forum tomorrow morning, you'll find a lot" Ay replied and Jemima chuckled realizing that they were already at the bar.

"So here's the bar here and feel free to ask for whatever you want" Ay said and Jemima nodded glancing at the bartender who looked too quiet and well hot for a bartender.

"Don't worry, he's not gonna do you anything" Ay added with an amused face catching how weird Jemima glanced at the bartender.

"Sorry" Jemima muttered embarrassed at her actions.

"Don't worry. It's totally fine. So I'll leave you in the hands of Isa and don't worry, you'll be fine" Ay said and before Jemima could mutter a thank you, he was gone from her field of view. Jemima sighed softly and turned to find a seat in front of the bartender who was now watching her quietly.

"Hi Isa" Jemima muttered, swallowing her saliva and the bartender nodded his head quietly.

"Hello Jemima" he greeted.

"So what do you want?" he asked.

"You know me?" Jemima asked for the hundredth time that night and Isa nodded his head.

"Why not?" he asked and Jemima nodded her head quietly.

"I see," she said under her breath.

"So what mocktail would you be going for?" Isa asked.

"Virgin Margarita, Virgin Mojito, Shirly Temple, Non alcoholic Mimosa, Virgin Cosmopolitan,Non alcoholic sangrin.." he reeled off and Jemima raised an eyebrow watching him.

"Shirly Temple please" Jemima replied with a small smile on her lips.

"Nice choice" Isa replied, moving towards the shelves behind him to make her mocktail.

"So how do you know me? I don't know you" Jemima asked.

"How many people are in the world Jemima?" Isa asked and Jemima shrugged her shoulders.

"Well tad over eight billion people as at last year" Isa replied and Jemima nodded her head again.

"So?" she asked.

"Well in a human being's lifetime, he or she has the opportunity to have acquaintances of about 1.5 million" Isa replied while Jemima folded her arms and her interest piqued.

"That many people?" she asked.

"Well I think some people get to know up to 2.5 million people" Isa replied and Jemima nodded.

"But according to some theories, over 10 million people could know you exist and you wouldn't know about it" Isa added and Jemima raised her eyebrow.

"Over ten million? Isn't that a bit far-fetched?" she asked.

"Doesn't that answer your question?" Isa asked in reply and Jemima, realizing why Isa had taken the time to explain such theories to her in the first place chuckled.

"Do you understand now?" he asked and Jemima nodded her head watching as he placed a tray of drink in front of her.

"Shirly Temple" he muttered and Jemima stretched her hand to take her drink, sipping out of it quietly. By the time she raised her head, Isa was already attending to someone else. She swirled her chair looking across the hordes of teenagers scattered through the party dancing and carrying cups, the cups had somehow turned out to be a necessity because Jemima hadn't even ran into someone that wasn't carrying a cup.

She scrolled through her Instagram feed slowly nodding her head to the background music. She quickly sent a text to Doyin asking her where she was. She was beginning to feel lonely and needed someone to talk to. After waiting for Doyin's reply for a few minutes and taking a few pictures of herself, she decided to find Doyin herself.

She got off the chair and was instantly jumped into someone spilling the rest of her mocktail on the stranger.

"Oh my, I'm so sorry" Jemima muttered, raising her head to meet a dark skinned boy glancing down at her with a small frown on his face. Her drink had spilled on the water round neck he had wore underneath his jean jacket.

"I'm sorry" Jemima muttered again wondering how the boy could look both Yoruba and Hausa to her at the same time.

"Oh it's fine" the boy said finally speaking and Jemima mentally gave her accolades for not just being able to pull of a Yoruba and Hausa look but being able to sound like he lived all his life in Europe.

"Are you sure?" she asked him hesitatingly and the boy turned to her chuckling and nodding his head.

"Yes, it is. You do look familiar by the way?" he said wearing a curious expression and Jemima dropped her head quietly chuckling.

"I spilled my drink on you and I am very sorry about that but you saying I look familiar the next second? You have to come up with something better" Jemima replied, pursing her lips.

"That's it. You are Jemima right?" he asked and Jemima instantly wanted to swallow the previous words she had said before back. The boy laughed watching Jemima's expression.

"Don't sweat it. Jeremiah would come for my head if I dared to make a move on his younger sister" he said and Jemima looked at him in surprise.

"You know my brother?" she asked and the boy nodded his head.

"Yes of course. I'm Sarki by the way" the boy replied, introducing himself in the process.

"Sarki?" Jemima asked, cocking her eyebrows.

"Yes. Sarki" Sarki replied, wearing an amused smile.

"And what's your name supposed to mean?" Jemima asked, wondering why on earth parents liked to embarrass their children by giving them super weird ass names. If her parents had given her some weird name like Sarki, she definitely wouldn't forgive them.

"One who has the name of a king," Sarki replied and Jemima chuckled, a small smile spreading across her lips..

"Wow. One who has the name of a king" Jemima repeated and Sarki nodded his head.

"That's sounds like something only the Hausa's would come up with" Jemima said and Sarki burst into laughter.

"You are right on point" Sarki replied and Jemima shrugged her shoulders.

"Figures"

"So your Mom is Yoruba?" Jemim asked and it was now Sarki's turn to cock his eyebrow.

"How did you know?"

"Your face. You have very distinctive Yourba and Hausa features, allow me to say a perfect mix. And then you said your name, Sarki. Your mom couldn't have been from Hausa land, her family wouldn't care what they named the child whether it was Hausa or Yoruba, as long as he had a nice name and they threw fancy parties, however the reverse is the case if your father is Hausa. The elders in the family would you know deliberate so nights before the birth of the child and after he or she is born, especially if the child is a boy and then bless him with a nice with meaning only them can give explanations to" Jemima replied sipping the rest of her Shirly Temple and dropping the empty cup on the table.

"It sure does run in the family" Sarki muttered laughing quietly.

"And hell yeah, you are right," he added, nodding his head.

"And the accent? You lived in Europe?" Jemima asked and Sarki shook his head.

"Baby girl, you are wrong on this one. I went to a European school in Abuja" Sarki replied and Jemima nodded her head.

"Nice to meet you Jemima, I once told Jeremiah to bring you home but he wouldn't even hear it" Sarki muttered laughing and shaking his head.

"Oh really?" Jemima asked, chuckling and nodding her head.

"Jemima!" someone hollered and Jemima found Bimbo in front of her grinning while holding a cup. The moment Bimbo grabbed her hand, she already knew the latter had been drinking but somehow wasn't drunk yet.

"Hi Sarki," Bimbo greeted with a grin.

"Hi Bimmy" Sarki greeted and Bimbo immediately made a pout.

"You clearly know that Jeremiah would come for your head and your entire being if he hears you"

"Well, he can't hear me," Sarki replied laughing and Bimbo shook her head, tightening her grip on Jemima's hands.

"Well I'm here to take Jemima to have fun. Byeee" Bimbo informed him, now waiting for either Sarki or Jemima to bid each other goodbye before pulling Jemima away.

"You are going to squeeze my nerves endings out of my skin if you grip me tighter" Jemima said and Bimbo chuckled instantly releasing her grip on Jemima's hand.

"Where have you been?" Jemima asked.

"I didn't know you also got an invitation," Jemima added.

"Heraline gave Jeremiah two and I didn't get mine until tonight" Bimbo replied.

"You know Heraline?" Jemima asked in surprise and Bimbo quickly shook her head.

"I don't know her personally but I think she worked with Jeremiah on a freelance modelling shoot and that's how they got acquainted" Bimbo replied and Jemima nodded her head.

"How come I've never heard of this before?" Jemima muttered underneath her breath and Bimbo swallowed her saliva.

"You knew Sarki?" Bimbo asked.

"Guess who I just saw?" Sarki asked grinning as he sat down and grabbed a cup downing some of the contents down his throat.

"Who?" one of the boys asked and Sarki turned to the boy seated beside Heraline still maintaining the grin on his face.

"Jeremiah's younger sister, Jemima" Sarki replied and the latter merely threw him a glance without saying anything.

"She's so cute and smart, it runs in the family," he added, turning his head and pointing towards where Bimbo and Jemima were standing.

"That's her, the one on the crop top," he said.

Everyone turned to glance at the duo but the only view they could get was the back of a mildly slim girl with her braids packed messily upwards but still in a fashionable way, a bit of her slim clean back and waist beads that rested on her waist like they were meant to be there.

Happy New Month peopleeeeeeeeee. Welcome to the month of freedom and in whatever it might be, I pray and hope that you are truly free even if it involves been free from Nigeria.

Like I promised last week, the updates will be back to been regular, twice a week, on Monday's and Friday's. Someone tried to bargain double updates with me because it's new month but I'll see if I can make it work but the chapter will be quite short but then, expect another update before Friday or on Friday.

I'll like to make a correction, Karami is Sarki, I sorta changed the name at the last minute, I really don't know why but please I want you guys to know that. Sarki is Karami, the name is just different.

Who can guess who Isa is? I already gave an hint in two chapters from here though. I'm not asking you to go back and read it o.

I hope you are all enjoying this book as much as I am enjoying this book because I'm literally holding myself back from spilling everything about this book. I know I don't write slow burn like this but you see this slow burn will be worth it and besides, the slow burn is only for a short while.

That been said, I wanted to inform y'all that I have a new book on my Goodnovel account since last month and don't worry it's not going to be paid until next month. So you get to enjoy the book and the updates till next month. Don't sleep on it!!!!!. If you are a fan of bad girl and introverted boy, this book is for you.

And I told you guys the last time that I'm cooking something for you guys and no one said anything like y'all didn't see it. Anyways, the food should be ready by the end of this month or the middle fo next month too. Keep your fingers crossed for all the goodies I'm saving for you guysss.

Love, Semiloore.

CHAPTER TEN

"She's been asking for you" the first boy said and Micah raised his eyebrows pursing from taking a sip of from the cup in his hands.

"She came around my block too" Heraline added, folding her arms and relaxing into her seat.

"So what's the fuss about?" Sarki asked.

"Then I saw Poison chatting with her some days after. I saw them about three times together" the first boy replied and Sarki raised his eyebrow nodding his head.

"She's not stupid or dumb" Sarki said while everyone around the table turned to him.

"Look; whatever the issue is, you guys get home and settle it. You are killing the whole vibe here okay?" Sarki continued.

"I came here to have fun, I don't care if you came here for some other reason so please don't ruin my fun" Sarki continued standing up from his seat and moving his body to the music.

"Sarki my guyyy" a guy greeted by slapping handshakes with him and they both exchanged a brief hug.

"How you dey now?" he asked.

"I dey" Sarki replied.

"I see as you dey follow one babe talk that time, I hear say na Jeremiah's sister be that" he said and Sarki chuckled quietly.

"Na Jeremiah sister be that, wetin happen?" Sarki asked.

"Ha, come help me run am now. The babe set gan, naso everybody just dey look am since morning. Heraline dey drag am everywhere nobody fit even near am say dem wan collect number, sha come help me run am fess before another person go jam am" the guy replied nudging Sarki on the shoulder playfully.

"Get lost" a voice drifted into both of them ears and Sarki turned to see Micah staring at the other guy with a straight face. The fact that his ears were still trembling from the voice told him that Micah had just spoken.

"King" the latter called bowing his head lightly.

"Didn't you hear me?" Micah asked.

"And tell your people, I see anybody near her, they are as good as dead" Micah added while everyone stared in shock and surprise.

"King" Heraline muttered and Micah rubbed his forehead.

"Where's Jeremiah?" he asked and Heraline swallowed her saliva. She Knew that tone all too well.

"I'll send for him," Heraline replied, pushing herself to her feet.

Everyone knew that Micah was more than pissed already and the fact he hadn't flung the cup of alcohol in his hands at someone was evidence that he wasn't fully angry yet. Jeremiah was Micah's school son. No one knew the story or how they had even come to be in the first place as everyone knew one fact, Jeremiah was a precious person to Micah.

And someone had gotten the guts from God knows where to come and ask Sarki for his younger sister's number in front of him even going ahead to clearly state that he had just wanted to mess with her. Everyone could feel the change of atmosphere immediately and in order to avoid being in the line of fire, they all kept quiet watching Micah sip from his drink and scroll through his phone without another word.

"Where's my brother?' Jemimah asked and Bimbo shrugged her shoulders.

"He's probably playing some games upstairs or around the pool side" Bimbo replied and Jemimah nodded her head scrolling through her phone as well. She had noticed a lot of people looking at her and even some of the guys urging each other to come and approach her and had somehow rehearsed ways and manners to turn each and every one of them down and then suddenly she realised that although the eyes on her didn't reduce, no one was trying to walk up to her or something.

"Isn't that enough alcohol for a night?" Jemimah asked and Bimbo glanced at the cup in her hands and shook her head.

"Don't worry about me, I know my limits" Bimbo replied and Jemimah nodded her head.

"Obviously" She replied genuinely surprised. Before Bimbo came to drag away from Sarki, her mouth was already smelling alcohol so she had guessed that she might have taken two cups before then and just during the time they had sat down to eat, Bimbo had taken another two yet her words were constructed perfectly like she hadn't taken any drink at all.

"Why are you looking at me like that?" Bimbo asked, standing up from collecting the tray of peppered chicken someone brought.

"My guts tell me you are thinking, where did Bimbo know how to drink and not get drunk?" Bimbo asked and Jemimah nodded her head.

"Then answer me" she replied, taking a chunk of the chicken wing and slipping into her mouth.

"I went with Jeremiah to this house party and he told me not to take any drinks, I somehow forgot that I got drunk and almost drugged. " Bimbo replied while Jemimah stared at her in surprise and shock.

"Jeremiah got quite pissed" Bimbo continued talking while tearing the chicken into two different plates.

"Made me come over one time and made me drink so many bottles, we did that for some four five times till I could drink a full bottle or even two and I wouldn't even get drunk" Bimbo finished slipping a chunk of chicken into her own mouth while Jemimah stared at her trying to process what Bimbo had just explained to her.

"Jeremiah said, he wouldn't always be there so I had to be capable of looking out for myself too" she added and Jemimah glared at her.

"I know okay! You don't have to remind me that you both love yourselves to death" she replied while Bimbo burst into laughter while Jemimah smiled to herself picking another chunk of chicken.

Jeremiah had always been like that; overly protective, in the confines of their secondary school, he could look after her without her knowing or anything but here in CUA, the story was different so he made himself admit that he couldn't be her superman everyday and so he had to teach her how to avoid trouble. Jemimah mentally gave her elder brother the award of boyfriend of the month.

So who's going to teach you how not to get drunk? her subconscious asked and Jemimah rolled her eyes while trying Doyin's number for the twentieth time that night.

"I have to find Doyin, I have been ringing her number since and she's not picking it, " Jemimah muttered pursing her lips.

"Let's find Heraline so she can ask them to find her," Bimbo replied, taking the last chunk of chicken and standing on her feet.

"I even forgot to ask Jemimah, did you dress like this to specifically seduce someone or what?' Bimbo asked playfully and Jemimah burst into laughter.

"I wish there was someone I could actually seduce" Jemima replied and both girls burst into laughter.

"But you do look really hot tonight" Bimbo commented again.

"Where's your phone?" she asked.

"Let me take full pictures of you" she added while Jemimah stretched her phone towards her.

Jemimah scrolled through the pictures throwing flying kisses towards Bimbo as they walked downstairs.

"Instagram worthy pictures, that's what I took, feed your eyes ehn" Bimbo boasted and the two girls burst into laughter again.

"Heraline" Jemiamh called as soon as they saw her.

"Have you seen my friend?" she asked and Heraline shook her head.

"They are already checking the third floor and CCTVs cameras, I feel like you'll disappear as soon as we find your friend" Heraline replied and Jemimah nodded her head.

"We stay in school hostels, the gates get locked by 12am," Jemimah replied.

"Let's take pictures before they find Doyin " Heraline said, bringing out her phone and pulling Doyin closer to her while they started posing and taking pictures.

"Hey baby" Heraline suddenly called out and Jemimah watched in amazement as Heraline rushed into the arms of someone raining kisses all over their face. Her eyebrows rigged together upon realising that Isa was the one Heraline was hugging.

"Who's Isa to Heraline?" Jemimah suddenly blurted out and Bimbo laughed.

"You just watched Heraline kiss him like that and you are asking what they are?"

"That's Heraline's boyfriend's baby girl, the only one capable of turning that girl into a clingy cat," Bimbo added and Jemimah chuckled.

Isa didn't know because of the universe whatever, he knew her because Heraline knew her. She chuckled lightly wondering how she had fallen for such gibberish.

"Helloooo " someone booed into Jemimah's ears and Jemimah turned to see someone holding a drunk Doyin. She quickly rushed over collecting Doyin from the stranger and wrapping her hands around her waist to steady.

"Jesus, Doyin, how much did you drink?" Jemimah asked and Doyin burst into laughter.

"I kept losing so I had no choice but to drink," she replied, her voice slurry and Jemimah shook her head, slipping her phone into her pocket.

"Your friend is drunk " Heraline muttered pursing her lips.

"Why don't you let Isa go and drop you guys?" Heraline asked and Jemimah raised her head to glance at Isa.

"You've met my boyfriend at the bar right?" Heraline asked with a grin and Jemimah nodded her head.

"Yes I did," she replied.

"Babe, where's your car keys?" Heraline turned to ask Isa who immediately slipped his hands into his pockets.

"Don't bother " Jemimah announced stopping the movements of the duo.

"The driver that brought us here is still waiting outside, " Jemimah added and Heraline raised her eyebrow.

"You had him wait?' Bimbo asked.

"I paid him to wait," Jemimah replied, turning to glance at Heraline again.

"Thank you very much for inviting us to your party, Hera. I enjoyed it and Doyin obviously enjoyed it too. Have a good night" Jemimah said, pulling Doyin with her while walking away. Bimbo watched Jemimah help a chattering to no end Doyin and turned to glance at Isa.

"And what did you say to Jemimah at the bar?" she asked and Isa furrowed his brows.

'What did you think I must have said to her?' Isa shot back and Bimbo shrugged her shoulders.

"If I had an idea I wouldn't ask you but I'll just let you both know in case Heraline doesn't have an idea, Jemimah hates a lot of stuffs, from random stuffs to a lot of things we could consider normal but there a top ten list that we all avoided in sec school" Bimbo replied.

"You went to the same sec school with Jemimah?" Herlaine asked and Bimbo chuckled.

"Stop asking me the obvious Hera, " Bimbo replied.

"Making a fool out of her, Jemimah hates it the most. Not the most but definitely in the top ten, she despises it." Bimbo added, shrugging her shoulders while picking another cup from a tray someone was passing around.

"I know Jeremiah didn't ask you to give Jemimah an invitation letter, he wouldn't. There was no way on earth he would have allowed it. But you found some way to make him busy that he barely remembered to ask you about it. For whatever reason you invited Jemimah to your party Heraline, I wish, I desperately wish you do not plan to include her into any of your clan cult games" Bimbo continued shaking her head and taking a sip.

"I desperately wish you do not plan to make her a chess player because Jemimah loves Chess and excels at it, she excels at everything, everything she ever tries. You would be throwing a stone on your foot if that's what you are planning" she finished raising her cup up.

"Nice party by the way" she muttered before flashing the duo a smile and walking away.

"You know I also wanted to ask Jumoke, why did you give her an invitation?"

Heraline turned to her boyfriend with an amused smile on her lips "Are you pretending not to know or you really do not know?" she asked and Isa chuckled.

"King is not going to spare you" Isa replied and Heraline chuckled.

"Even if I had a thousand lives, I wouldn't cross him" Heraline replied, wrapping her hands around Isa's waist and standing on her toes to press her lips against Isa's but the latter turned his face to the side just in time.

"What did you say to Jemimah huh?" Heraline asked unsurprised that Isa had turned his face.

"A joke that turns out after all is not that funny" Isa replied with furrowed brows.

"We'll find her later and apologise" Heraline muttered quietly reaching for Isa's lips again and this time around he didn't turn his head. Wrapping her hands around his neck, she kissed him fervently like her life depended on it.

"Fucking get a room!"

Hello guysssss; I deeply apologize for being such a pain in the ass by not updating for a full week even after I promised extra chapters. It was really inevitable but here I am with another update and don't worry. I have the updates for this week already all I need to do on Friday is to click on publish so don't worry about updates for this week.

This chapter will be needed a later part of the book so make sure you don't forget this part. I'm curious because of the suspense in this chapter. I have no idea what Bimbo was talking to Heraline and Isa about, I'm even further confused on what Isa was talking to Heraline about. All in all, I know I'm in for some really dirty games, not me per say, y'all.

Who likes Isa?

And the part where Bimbo told Jemima how Jeremiah made her learn how to drink is the sweetest part of this chapter. Jeremiah is still a sweet human being.

Thank you for the 2K reads and 1k votes. Lots of love, I've resumed posting and being active on my writing IG page and just go there out the new updates. You don't want to miss any of them. I also hope you don't.

11 ' ELEVEN '

Pulling a drunk Doyin with her as she walked outside gave off a funny impression as the latter kept walking fast or too slow and twice almost tumbled them both together.

By the time they were outside the party; Jemima brought out her phone again to glance at the message that buzzed on her phone earlier. The Bolt driver had left; she doubted if the school security would even allow private cars into the school by that time.

Only students with influence or school transportation which will never be available would be allowed into the school premises. For a moment, Jemima regretted letting her anger get the better part of her, Isa would have no problem driving them to the hostel.

"You know; I didn't even know who the first President of Nigeria was?" Doyin continued blabbering and Jemima chuckled.

"You didn't know?" She asked eyeing Doyin before shaking her head. She glanced at her phone again to see another message from Peter asking them if they had gotten back to the hostel yet. She was intentionally ignoring his messages because she knew she would be putting the twins into a state of worry by telling them their predicament.

If she was all by herself, or if Doyin wasn't drunk; they could have come up with ways to get back to the hostel but with Doyin being unable to stand by herself or even think reasonably; there was no way they would get back to the hostel without external help.

"Hey Jemima!" Someone called and Jemima turned to see a familiar face. She didn't even realize a helpless smile had crawled up her lips.

"Abraham" she greeted smiling.

"What are you doing here?" He sled leaning over and giving her a small hug.

"My bolt driver betrayed me" Jemima replied wearing a mournful face and Black burst into laughter.

"Let me be a reliable bolt driver," he replied, winking at her while shaking his head.

"Your friend certainly doesn't know how to hold her alcohol" he muttered and Jemima rolled her eyes laughing.

"I didn't know why she chose to play some stupid games in the first place" Jemima replied pulling Doyin with her while wincing. Without another word; Black reached for Doyin and carried her in a bridal style walking in clear steps towards the car.

Surprised for a moment, Jemima quickly jogged up to him chuckling lightly.

"How much do you work out?" She asked falling into steps beside Black as he stopped beside a Black Rangerover.

"The key is in my left pocket," Black replied, turning his left pocket towards her. Jemima nodded her head, slipping her hands into his pockets and bringing out the keys and unlocking the car. Black carefully placed an already dozing Doyin at the back seat.

Both Doyin and Black got into the front seat and driver's seat and Black started the car reversing out of the car park into the Main Street.

"A lot, I work out a lot" Black replied and Jemima nodded her head.

"I envy you" Jemima muttered laughing and texting Peter who had sent about five more messages that they were on their way back to the hostel.

"I didn't know you got invited to Heraline's party" Jemima started trying to start a conversation.

"I did get invited but I just came to drop someone off" Black replied.

"King?" Jemima asked with an eyebrow raised and Black burst into laughter.

"How did you know?" He asked with an amused face.

"A guess. I remember you mentioning me the last time you picked me up" Jemima replied and the latter nodded his head.

"You guys are so alike, you remember the most smallest of things"

"So King was at the party?" Jemima asked and Black nodded his head glancing at Jemima with a puzzled face.

Did she even have any idea who King was? Who he was?

"Yup," Black replied.

Jemima nodded her head regretting she hadn't run into Black earlier. For someone with such a voice; he definitely had to have a nice face to go with it. She had seen her fair share of handsome guys in CUA and a lot more at Heraline's party but none of them appealed to her.

She just wanted to find someone she would deem attractive but apparently the person was yet to drop from heaven. Sewa and Farida still ridiculed her high tastes two days before and told her God got tired of sending her handsome guys that's why she hasn't found someone attractive.

Jemima swallowed her saliva as soon as they reached the school gates and there were a few cars lined up while the school security checked and searched the cars. Jemima pursed her lips wondering what lie they would cook up for the securities; there was no way Black would be able to convince them but as she was thinking, she realized that Black didn't bother joining the line of waiting card and directly drove into the school and not even one security came forward to stop him, they even seemed to salute the car.

She stared at Black in shock and surprise, the look on Jemima's face gave Black the reply to the question he had asked himself before.

She had no idea. Jeremiah didn't tell her and somehow, she was oblivious to it too.

A smile spread across Black lips "Why are you looking at me like that?" He asked.

"Those security guys didn't stop us? They even saluted the car, right?" Jemima asked and Black laughed again.

"Don't think too much; a member of the SUG owns this car, the security guards are very much familiar with it and that's what they saluted.

"Oh" Jemima replied, chuckling.

"That's why you didn't wound down the glass at all" Jemima added and Black nodded his head taking another glance at Jemima.

He definitely couldn't be the one to break the news to her, who they were? What they were, it wasn't up to him but he was sure that whenever she found out.... He really didn't want to know.

He stopped directly in front of their hostel and Jemima was surprised to see both Paul and Peter waiting. Both boys rushed towards them.

"Why did it take so long for you to reply to your messages?" Peter asked with a frown and Jemima pouted.

"I'm sorry" she replied, helping Black grab an already asleep Doyin.

"She drank?" Paul asked grabbing Doyin and hugging her to prevent her from falling.

"How did you know?" Jemima asked, turning to Black.

"Thank you so much Abraham. I'll treat you next time" She said, thanking him with a grin and Black winked at her.

"Then you owe me" he replied, closing the distance between them and giving her a small hug.

Black raised his head to meet the faces of the two boys standing next to Jemima. They both had surprised looks on their faces but they weren't saying anything.

They recognized him. They knew who he was, if they knew; how on earth did Jemima have no idea?

"Bye bye" Jemima said, waving at Black as he got into the car and reversed before driving off.

"Who was that?" Peter asked.

"Abraham?" Jemima asked.

"Abraham?" Peter asked.

"Yes. Everyone else knows him as Black, he's one of Jeremiah's close friends" Jemima replied as a loud siren filled their ears.

"Oh my god, just put Doyin on my back, the hostel will soon be locked" Jemima said in a rush while bending her back.

"Can you carry her?" Peter asked with concern.

"Just two floors, I can manage," Jemima replied, hurrying them up while glancing at the hostel gates that had both boys and girls rushing into their hostels.

"Byeeee" Jemima cooed to the boys wincing as she carried Doyin into the hostel.

"You exercise?" Jemima asked the sleeping girl behind her.

"You fucking liar, if you did any work out, how are you this heavy?" She continued asking while climbing the stairs, her breaths labored.

It was futile to try to go to Doyin's room which was even farther. She rushed to her room and kicked the door twice, she gave a small smile to Vickie who had opened the door for her.

She threw Doyin on her bed panting slightly at the extreme work out she had just done.

"Is the party finished?" Vickie asked Jemima handling her a bottle of water.

Jemima stared at both Vickie and the bottle of water with sheer confusion and surprise. Vickie had never made an attempt to even have a conversation with her before.

Was that how badly she was pained at not being invited to Heraline's party?

"No" Jemima replied, collecting the bottle of water from her and Vickie nodded her head walking back to her bunk and climbing onto her bed. Jemima watched her grab her iPad and continue whatever she was doing on it before she walked in. She cocked her eyebrow as she took her tenth gulp of the water, she thought Vickie would want to know everything that went down at the party, but she wasn't asking anything.

Hello guyssssss, see this time around I kept to my promise. I've started working on another chapter because ASUU has called off strike and I'm resuming next week Monday. And what's more? My exams are to start on 7th of next month so updates might come once in a week or not at all but I'll try my best to keep up.

Who else is curious of what Jemima's reaction will be when she realizes who King and Black is? Paul and Peter obviously recognizes him and Jemima is the new clueless in form of an human.

Spam with votes and comments. Lots of love.

12 | TWELVE

Despite the fact she was tired, Jemima found herself scrolling through her phone for the next three hours. She was shocked when she got an Instagram notification that Heraline had tagged her. She clicked on the post and surprise fitted across her face seeing that Heraline had posted several pictures about the party, there were two pictures of her and Herlaine and there were already over hundred comments in less than three minutes of making the post. One could easily say they had been waiting for her to make the post.

She chuckled upon realising that a lot of people were making comments about her and dropping all sorts of compliments, feeling giddy, she posted the slide containing her and Heraline to her story and tagged her. Heraline immediately made the post to her story and within minutes, Jemima found her follower count increasing and message requests popping on her screen.

Ignoring most of the requests, she went ahead to take a short bath at past 2am in the morning. She brought out new bedsheets from her wardrobe and spread them on the floor before lying on them and covering herself. She didn't have to whisper to the goddess of sleep before she took her away.

Doyin was the one who had woken her up the next morning, they had both dressed up amidst bants and jests, and rushed for their first early morning class. No matter the face she made, Paul or Peter, especially Peter didn't smile at her. By the time the lecturer was leaving the class, Doyin quickly blocked the twins' passway pouting.

"I didn't know I was going to get that drunk easily" Doyin whined and Paul scoffed.

"You didn't know? Do yin, how many times have you actually had access to alcohol?" Paul asked.

"How many drinks or rather how many cups did you have and you didn't realise that you were going to get drunk?" Paul asked again.

"I'm sorry okay" Doyin replied, apologising and grabbing Peter's hands, swinging it like a small child.

"Peter say something, " she whined. The latter turned to her with a scowl.

"What if something had happened to you?" Peter asked and Doyin sighed softly.

"I'm really sorry. I just wanted to play games and...." Doyin tried to reply but Peter cut her off amidst her reply.

"Play games with strangers and have fun at someone's party whom you've never had a conversation with before" Peter muttered.

"Jemima was there so I ended up fine okay" Doyin repleid and Peter scoffed again.

"What if she drank too? What did you think would happen to you two?" Peter asked and Doyin sighed again throwing playful punches to Peter while pouting.

"Peter, I turned out fine okay" Doyin replied in a small voice and Paul waved his phone at the two girls.

"Well ButterFly Fairy made a post and there was you Doyin playing games and drinking and Jemima talking to Isa and some other pictures, pictures of Jemima carrying you into the hostel and pictures of Jemima carrying you at the party while talking to Isa and Heraline" Paul announced and Jemima winced.

"What the ..." she muttered, unable to finish her statement while collecting Paul's phone and scrolling through the post.

"Heck, I didn't even know who Isa was until Bimbo mentioned who he was, what does this goddamn bastard mean by I tried to fit in?" Jemima asked, giving Paul back his phone and rubbing her forehead. Doyin, who had also brought out her phone and was also reading the post, chuckled.

"That's what you get for playing games with strangers" Peter started.

"Imagine a total idiot who doesn't even know you writing some jargons online" He added and Jemima rubbed her forehead.

"Whoever this Butterfly Fairy is, he or she is starting to get on my nerves" Doyin replied with a frown.

"Look Paul, Doyin was wrong for drinking and playing games with strangers but it's really alright, at least she was fine when I found her and she's still fine now" Jemima said and Peter shrugged his shoulders.

"I know, I was just really worried last night. " Peter replied and Jemima winked at him.

"We are fine as you can see," Jemima said, bringing out her phone to show off the nice compliments she had gotten under Heraline's posts.

"So Heraline made several posts about her party yesterday and I was in two slides, you need to see how everyone was fawning over me" Jemima started laughing playfully while clicking on Heraline's posts. A small frown greased her face as she scrolled through the comment section.

"What's going on?" Doyin asked, peering into her phone.

"The comments are gone, " Jemima replied.

"Gone?" Paul asked and Jemima nodded, scrolling through her gallery and showing Doyin and the boys a screenshot of the comments she had taken the day before.

"What's going on?" Doyin asked.

"The comments about you were actually deleted, " she added and Jemima suddenly chuckled.

"I feel like this is Jeremiah's work. He doesn't let so many people look at his younger sister" Jemima said and Peter laughed.

"Then he has some serious sister complex" Peter said and Jemima nodded her head laughing.

"I can assure you that he definitely has it. " Jemima replied, agreeing as she closed her Instagram app and shook her head. She quickly sent Jeremiah a message attaching the post before and the screenshot she had taken.

"You are sending him a message?" Paul asked and Jemima asked.

"Grab your bag, we have another class at Prof Henry's LT" Paul announced and Jemima nodded, stretching her hand to pick her bag but Peter was faster than her, picking up the bag and slinging it over his shoulders easily.

"Boyfriend material, 1000 yards" Jemima hollered and both her and Doyin burst into laughter while the twins merely glanced at each other and shook their heads.

"I'm also sending a message to the family group to tell my parents that my elder brother is seriously ruining my chances of finding a boyfriend, " Jemima said laughing while the trio behind her paused in their steps. Jemima was quick to notice they had stopped and turned to them with raised eyebrows.

"What's going on?" she asked.

"What did you say just now?" Paul asked.

"I said I was going to send a message to the family group and tell my parents, my elder brother is ruining my chances of getting a boyfriend, " Jemima replied.

"You know getting the comments off Heraline's post" she added.

"Wow" Doyin breathed and Jemima folded her arms.

"What's wow?" Jemima asked.

"Your parents' baby girl" Peter replied.

"Your parents are amazing people" he added and Jemima chuckled a huge smile spreading all over her face.

"They are twice as amazing than you think they are"

Hello guysssssss; who missed meeeeeee? I missed reading you guys comments and you guys tooo. FUTA is pinning my neck against the wall and

I absolutely have no idea how I made time to write this. I hope you forgive me for the chapter being short.

My exams start next week as long ASUU doesn't go on strike with their new found issue with FG; I'm tired of these people. And if they do; all the best to them, me gan I'm tired.

You guys who claimed that Doyin is ButterFly Fairy; I'm waiting for your conjectures on this one. And I'm also curious about who deleted Jemima's comments under Heraline's post.

Wish me luck and I love you guysss.

<h1 style="text-align:center">13 | THIRTEEN |</h1>

J emimah scrolled through her phone, barely taking into notice; her environment. She had to admit; the school forum was quite an addicting place and shockingly very informative, you could easily find anything concerning anybody including the lecturers there. Jemima didn't know why she was looking for information on Isa and Heraline.

And the school forums somehow didn't have enough information, the only information she could get was that Isa and Heraline were deeply in love and had been dating since their first year at Crest; another post said they had been dating way before they both got into Crest and even had pictures of the younger duo pressing their heads together to the post.

Jemimah scroll further down the posts, Heraline and Isa weren't ordinary students of CUA, they could be cultists or affiliated with them because if the family history of the current Vice Chancellor of the school could be found on the school forum; who was Isa and Heraline that barely important information was found on them.

She clicked her tongue lightly while closing the forum and replying to the texts she was yet to respond to on her iMessage. Her phone almost started ringing immediately and a smile wore its way to her face after seeing the caller ID. She picked up the call and pressed the phone to her ears.

"Where are you?' Jeremiah asked.

"I'm walking back to my hostel; I wanted to check something on my phone so I took a pause around the Faculty of Theatre Arts and I'm walking back already" Jemimah replied.

"Oh. maybe I'll come to your hostel area tonight, " Jeremiah replied, and the latter chuckled.

"That reminds me, what do you mean by I'm ruining your chances of finding a boyfriend?" Jeremiah asked with laughter in his voice.

"You asked Heraline to take down the comments of me under her post" Jemimah replied fake sulking even though she knew Jeremiah couldn't see her.

"What comments? Did Heraline make a post?" Jeremiah asked, puzzled.

"Wait a minute, you attended her party?" Jeremiah asked again leaving Jemimah dazed.

'What do you mean by I attended her party? I thought you asked her to give me an invitation card" Jemimah shot back.

"Me? I would never agree to that" Jeremiah replied.

"What do you mean?"

"First, what comments were you talking about?" Jeremiah asked.

"Well Heraline and I took a few pictures at the party and there were so many comments asking about who I was after she posted it because I was really pretty; I even took a screenshot but the next day, the comments were gone. All of them, in fact, if I didn't think of a screenshot, one might as well accuse me of lying" Jemima replied, rolling her eyes.

"Send me the screenshots, I haven't opened my gram in a while. I'll check on Hera's post myself" Jeremiah replied.

"So you didn't ask Heraline to give me an invitation card?" Jemimah asked.

"I did. I just remembered that she asked if you would like to attend and I nodded my head. I was doing something else so I just forgot" Jeremiah replied and Jemimah burst into laughter.

"You are getting old" She joked and Jeremiah laughed lightly.

"I'll call you when I get to your hostel tonight," He added.

"Okay. I also want to ask you something too" Jemimah replied.

"Oh. Okay. Love you"

"I love you too"

Jemimah ended the call with a furrow of her brows. If Jeremiah didn't ask Heraline to delete the comments under her post, who could have asked her to? Or did Heraline delete them by herself? There were other pictures that Heraline took with other people and there were comments about them, the comments still remained in the comments section. She was the only one whose comments were gone. She had the urge to ask Heraline why it was so but she decided in another split second that she wasn't going to. Jeremiah was going to find out and whenever and whatever he found out, he was going to let her know.

She slipped her phone into her pocket and almost immediately buzzed. She brought out her phone and there was a new notification on the school forum by ButterFly Fairy. She clicked on the post that was already gaining a whole lot of traction and rolled her eyes.

"What exactly is this girl's problem? Why can't she let people be for goodness sake!" Jemimah exclaimed, her face morphing into a frown while scrolling through the post.

"What if she has a Sugar Daddy? What does it have to do with you?" Jemimah asked no one in particular as she continued walking towards the hostel. She closed the school forum, placing the phone into her tote bag and folding her arms.

Jemimah had always been the type of mind her business, she didn't know if it was hereditary or something their parents had unconsciously passed to them. She and Jeremiah never poked nose in what was not their business, if given permission, they sometimes interfered but it was so rare not to gossip about something else.

But this ButterFly Fairy human being went to lengths, photographing people and making defamatory posts about them. It wasn't a problem when she first saw her posts, Jemimah had thought that she was very nosey but barely two weeks later, she already had over 200 posts of different people on the campus. No one knew where she was gathering her information or who she or he was but everyone scrambled to her page and she was already beginning to be addressed as the top gossip blogger making every other top blogger on the forum uncomfortable.

Jemimah did not like the fact that someone was at liberty of exposing people's private dealings that had nothing to do with her online. But there was nothing she could do about it, the dastard had even gone ahead to make a post about her and Doyin. Her phone buzzed in her bag loudly and Jemimah rolled her eyes bringing out her phone.

It was Doyin who had sent her a message. She had sent her two links, a link to the post Butterfly Fairy had made and a link to a live. Jemimah tapped on the live and sighed.

"I knew she wouldn't seat down back just like that"

"I knew she wouldn't seat down back just like that"

14 | FOURTEEN |

"Hi guys; it's your girl Anna. It's been a while. I hope you guys didn't miss me that much" Jemima immediately fixed her Air-Pods trying to hear clearly whatever the girl in the video was trying to say.

"I'm sorry that I haven't made any posts since I resumed school and I didn't think I was going to in a while until I got numerous spam messages to a link of a post on my school forum. Nobody has to tell me that this post is trending. Someone took a picture of me getting down from a private car and made a post about me having a sugar Daddy" the girl in the video continued, she spoke with one of her slumped and the other hand doing something no one could see.

She looked way too relaxed for someone who had just been accused of having a Sugar Daddy. If the runouts went stronger and went viral; her career was somehow going to take a huge hit. So Jemimah had no idea why and how Annabelle could look so relaxed but then ever since she had known Annabelle as a model; she had proved over time that she wasn't like everyone else.

"I'm first mortified that Butterfly Fairy thinks that I'm not rich enough to afford a Toyota Venza Limited with my own money and I can only get a sugar Daddy who has it" Annabelle added a small smile at the edge of her lips.

"I was smiling at the person in the car?" She asked and Jemima rolled her eyes. What if she was smiling? She wished people would just shut up their mouths already. She had already found her seat in one of the cemented chairs at the Faculty of Theater Arts.

"I can't smile at my Sugar Daddy no more? If I don't smile at him, how is he going to give me the car?" Annabelle asked and Jemimah burst into laughter.

"And if anyone wants to also get a car; I don't mind sharing my Sugar Daddy. I don't think he minds too. Or Lashe do you mind?" Annabelle asked turning the video camera to show a male figure at the other end of the room with a small frown on his face.

His handsome face was marred with a small frown and then he chuckled.

"I mind" he replied and the video camera returned to Annabelle's face.

"You heard the man; he minds" Annabella added laughing.

The live exploded. Jemimah remained dazed for seconds before dropping her head and bursting into laughter. There was practically no one who didn't know Lashe. One of the top teen models and singers in Africa and in recent times was gaining very crazy traction in other continents.

Nobody would have imagined that Annabella and Lashe were friends. And even close ones at that, Lashe had personally come to drop Annabelle at school.

"There are too many messages; I can't see them so I can't answer" Annabelle continued her face unchanging and remaining as relaxed as when she had first started the live. It was as though she hadn't just dropped the Bomb of the Month or even maybe the year.

"Lashe is too young to be my sugar Daddy?" Annabelle asked.

"He doesn't mind and neither does Ibukunoluwa mind. I'm a sweet side chick so she really, really likes me" Annabelle replied and Jemimah laughed again.

"She really, really is crazy" she muttered quietly while she continued watching Annabelle answer some random questions. She didn't have to close the live to know that people were already going over to roast ButterFly Fairy.

And her thoughts were further confirmed when Annabelle's live ended and she opened the school forum. ButterFly Fairy's profile was filled with numerous insults and sarcastic comments. It was the first time that 'he or she' had made a post and the subject of the post had made a counter; a counter that swept everyone off their feet and slapped him or her hard in the face.

ButterFly Fairy was already getting on a lot of people's nerves and seeing him or her getting slapped; there was no way they were going to let him or her go free. Jemimah scrolled through the comments snickering quietly. It was good that she was taught a lesson in such a style that only Annabelle could have come up with.

Even the internet wasn't spared; Twitter hashtags and trending were about Annabelle's live. Short clips were flying everywhere and Jemimah had a small smile on her lips as she resumed walking towards the hostel. For some reason, she felt good that Butterfly Fairy's face her has gotten slapped and got slapped real hard.

By the time Jemimah was walking into the hostel; Doyin was already waiting for her at the door of the room holding her stomach and laughing.

"Annabelle is such a nasty person," Doyin said as soon as she saw Jemimah.

"You need to have seen my face when she said Lashe was her Sugar Daddy. She just had to slap Butterfly Fairy across the face and I loved it" Jemimah replied opening the door to the room. The girls in the room went silent as soon as Jemimah stepped into the room.

More than used to it; Jemimah and Doyin barely paid them any attention.

"But why is she targeting Annabelle over and over again? It's like her third post of Annabelle" Doyin said slumping onto Jemimah's bed.

"Annabelle has been getting a lot of bad PR since last year; it's a miracle how she has managed to keep some of her modeling deals. Whatever ButterFly Fairy is doing is ruining her chances of ever making a comeback. Do you think someone paid ButterFly Fairy to do that?" Jemimah asked while carefully placing her sandals back on her shoe rack.

"You have a point but it's not like Annabelle was a good person to start with" Doyin replied.

"We barely know her. Who are we to be the judge of that?" Jemimah asked stretching back to her full length as she continued talking; "Besides; Lashe's presence in her live today is already more than a comeback for her. I still find it hard to believe that Lashe and Annabelle are close; like that close for her to call him her sugar Daddy on a live"

"I mean unless something else happens; She has successfully won the most unpredictable model of the year" Doyin announced.

"Annabelle had never been predictable," someone said and both girls turned to the three girls seated on the other side of the room.

"Are you talking to us?" Jemimah asked surprised.

"Yes"

Hello guysss, who missed meeeee? I had already published the last chapter before I remembered that I didn't add a note at the end. I wanted to post something on my page but I somehow forgot. I am very sorry for not keeping to my promise of one chapter per week last month but that would change this month. School is threatening to take my life with 8-6 everyday classes but my God is bigger than FUTA. I also want to thank the people who sent me emails and messages on Instagram; you guys are so caring and kind that it brings tears to my eyes. I wasn't supposed to say this yet but I'm cooking a surprise for y'all and you'll get to see it on my birthday which is 54 days from today. So keep your fingers crossed for both my surprise and Holding You Toght because the drama is about to get a little bit serious and we'll start to see more of my baby boy an other charactersssss. If you got confused about who Lashe is, then I'll take it that you haven't read STARS IN THE NIGHT SKY, and that only means one thing, you are missing out. Again.

See you soon dearies, I love you all so much. Let's bring HYT to 4k reads before the next update. Love you all.

15 FIFTEEN

J emimah slowly closed the door of her wardrobe turning to Vickie, she chuckled as she pointed to her and Doyin again.

"Are by any chance talking to us?" She asked and Vickie folded her arms chuckling.

"Who else would be talking to?" Vickie asked.

"Annabelle is not a respecter of anyone. She has always been like that, from Day one, she's arrogant and very prideful if you ask me, that's part of her whole person and I absolutely love it" Vickie continued.

"If you were a fan of Annabelle, seeing Lashe on her live wouldn't be such a big deal for you, late last year, Lashe and Ibukun went on a trip to Hauwei, there was always a third person with them but she was always blurred out. There were rumours it was Harriet or Annabelle but the media, your lovely media, disgusting tiny bloggers like ButterFly Fairy, for goodness sake, she's just a campus blogger, why is she acting like GossipMilli?' Vickie asked no one in particular before shaking her head.

"Well, back to what I was saying, the media immediately ruled out the fact that Lashe and Ibukun would have anything to do with Annabelle, but as a faithful and loyal fan of Annabelle, I knew she was the one. Harriet isn't as tall as she is and the fashion sense of the person in the blurred pictures had a large disparity to Harriet's" Vickie finished shrugging her shoulders.

"You are really an Annabelle stan" Doyin muttered staring at Vickie in surprise while Jemimah nodded her head. It was the first time she was seeing Vickie talk too much, most of the time even though she was there, the other girls did the talking.

"What are we going to do about PHY 101 abeg?" Doyin asked as soon as Vickie withdrew back to her bed.

"I no understand shingbain in that thing" Doyin cried out and Jemima burst into laughter.

"Let's see how our day goes tomorrow" Jemima replied and Doyin nodded her hug wrapping her hands around Jemima.

"You are a lifesaver" she whispered and Jemima laughed.

"You'll sell me for food" Jemimah argued back and they both burst into laughter.

"I need to finish some stuff in my room," Doyin said and Jemima nodded her head.

"I'll come back later" Doyin added while Jemima waved to her watching as she stepped out of the room.

Jemima had barely sat on her bed when her phone buzzed. It was a message from Jeremiah.

Mom came by, she was in a hurry and she dropped your stuff at my place, you can come at pick it up after your classes tomorrow. Love you so much.

Jemima chuckled, her provisions and foodstuffs were indeed running out and she had texted her mom to notify her. She had also forgotten that her mom said she was going to branch by the school and see them. It was more than obvious that something happened at the company so she had to rush back. She quickly texted her brother to let him know she got his message.

Jemima was spending more than enough time on the school forum, CUA indeed was the school to a lot of celebrities, as for why some teenage celebrities let all the private universities in Lagos, Ibadan, and Ogun state and came to Akure to school was a pure mystery to her.

She kept running into profiles and posts of different people and the school forum was more like a mini Instagram except that only the student of CUA was on it. Whoever had come up with the school forum; Jemima just had to give it to the person, a smart ass wouldn't be enough to describe the person.

A pure genius.

That was what the person was.

Jemima furrowed her bros upon stumbling upon a profile; it was a blank profile with zero posts but somehow had over ten thousand followers which Jemima deduced was more than half of the school.

O. Micah.

She scrolled upwards and downwards but there was nothing on the page. Curious she quickly took a screenshot of the profile and sent it to their group tagging Paul and Peter, the duo seemed to know everyone and everybody. Her brows were further furrowed when she Paul replied almost immediately.

We'll see in school immediately.

Chuckling lightly, she soon realized that there had to be some very interesting gist about this person, maybe he was some big teenage celebrity she had not taken notice of. Her mind went to Vickie's evaluation of Annabelle and she couldn't help but chuckle. It was nice to see that she still had fans who stood behind her.

#############

Jemima folded her arms, her eyes running across the twins in front of her, "So who is going to tell me who this O Micah is?"Jemima asked.

"I figured out he must be some hot shot but no one is coming to my head or no one came to my head rather" Jemima continued.

"Ever heard of the Titans?" Paul asked and Jemima furrowed her brows.

"Isn't that one of the cults y'all talked about? The one who killed people without batting an eyelash?" Jemima asked and Peter nodded.

"Yeah, yeah"

"This O Micah guy is one of them?"Jemima asked again.

"One of them would be an understatement" Paul replied and Jemima folded her arms.

"I like this, I like this. Tell me moreee" she cooed and Peter shook his head.

"No one addresses him as Micah, his full name is Obaniyi Micah but everyone calls him King" Peter started and Jemima burst into laughter.

"King as in, a literal King?" she asked wearing an amused look while staring from Paul to Peter.

"Yes. He's the leader of the Titans" Peter replied and Jemima suddenly felt a chill down her spine.

"Leader? Wow, that's nuts" she commented.

"Do you have any idea of how he became the leader?" Paul asked and Jemima shifted uncomfortably in her seat.

"How?" she asked quietly.

"He stabbed the former leader, that was when he had just entered the 100 level" Paul replied and Jemima stared at him mouth agape.

"There were series of cultist fights back then, some refused to take him as the leader and off with their heads" Paul added and Jemima's hands flew to her mouth. It wasn't the first time she was hearing how deadly the cultists in CUA were but just one person couldn't be this deadly.

"He's one person you shouldn't mess with if you love your life but you don't have that problem to deal with" Peter muttered a sleazy smile on his face while Jemima dropped her hands slowly.

"That's quite terrifying" she replied quietly shaking her head.

"Where's Doyin?" Paul asked and Jemima shrugged her shoulders.

"She wasn't in class when the lecturer left. Maybe she had something urgent to take care of" Jemima replied checking her wristwatch.

"I have to pick something at my brother's place outside school. I'll see you guys later" Jemima announced throwing flying kisses at the two boys who burst into laughter at her actions.

Paul watched Jemima walk out of the lecture theatre with an amused smile on his face "Is her pretense really good or she's really ignorant?" he asked and Peter chuckled.

"Ignorance could cost her life you know" he replied and Paul laughed.

"I don't think so, she was under their protection the moment she stepped into CUA"

"And she has no idea"

"What do you she's going to do when she finds out?" Peter asked and Paul smiled broadly.

"Jemima had always been a bundle of surprises, I can't wait to find out"

By the time the bike man dropped Jemima in front of Jeremiah's lodge, it was already nearing evening. But despite that, the people wandering around the street were very few, unlike the other areas that had student lodges, the street where Jeremiah's lodge was; was too quiet.

From the very first time she had visited him, she had noticed that it had been too quiet, Jeremiah had told her a very quiet person and someone who loved silence owned the street. The students were always thoroughly accessed before allowing them permission to live in the lodges. It wasn't just enough that you had money, you had to fit into the criteria.

It was no surprise that although it wasn't the most expensive, it was the most sought-after lodge in the school area. She wore a smile at the gateman, letting herself through the gate and walking straight to Jeremiah's door, even though there were several rooms in the compound, there was no soul in sight. It didn't come as a surprise to Jemima though.

By the time she was standing in front of the door, Jemima realized that she had forgotten the spare key to Jremiah's house in the hostel, to be specific, she had changed the tote bags she was carrying at the last minute so the key was in the former bag. She sighed and rubbed her forehead tired from the day's lectures and from the fact that her trip was in vain. She quickly dialled Jeremiah's number. The latter picked up on the second ring.

"Jemima, what's up?" Jeremiah greeted and Jemima sighed into the phone.

"I'm in front of your house right now and I realized that I forgot the key to your place in the hostel" Jemima whined while Jeremiah burst into laughter.

"I specifically told you not to forget"

"I changed bags last minute so I left it in the other bag"

"Wait a bit, I'll ask someone to send you another spare key"

"You gave someone else your spare key?" Jemima asked in surprise.

"Just wait a bit" Jeremiah replied before ending the call.

Jemima stared at her phone chuckling and wondering who else asides she and Bimbo would have Jeremiah's apartment spare key.

Jemima didn't have to wait up to ten minutes when she heard the sound of a car, since the compound and everywhere were so silent, the sound of a car parking just outside the gate was too loud to be ignored. She had crouched down in front of Jeremiah's door waiting.

The gate opened and her eyes widened as someone stepped into the compound and started walking toward her. Without thinking, Jemima had stretched to her full length staring without restraint, for some reason she recognized the figure, it was the person's back and side view whom she had found so attractive at Heraline's party. Staring at his full brows and lips drew into a thin line, Jemima was at a loss for words.

"Jemima?' he asked and Jemima found her throat dry upon recognizing the voice. It was the guy who had called Abraham the first time they met, he was the reason she started considering adding a deep baritone voice to the things she wanted in a boyfriend. She blinked her eyes uncontrollably a small smile spreading across her face.

"It's you"

Happy new month peopleeeeee. Welcome to my monthhhh, hehe. How are you all doing? Thank you so much for the care and love you send to me through mails and texts on IG, they mean so much to me.

I hate to be the bearer of bad news but updates on Holding You Tight will be becoming very slower than before. Although I will try to upload chapters every month I cannot make any promises that being said, my surprise for y'all on my Birthday still stands, keep your fingers crossed for it.

Will start dropping snippets on my IG account very very soon so stay glued to your phones. Let's get the comments to 1k and the reads to 5k. I've heard questions about why some characters have not shown their faces; you all will have to be patient to savour this meal, so just keep your fingers crossed.

My chest is doing anyhow, my babies are finally meetingggggg, hehe. I love you guys so much. See you soon, maybe an update would drop on my birthday, and maybe not.

Byeeeeeee

16 | SIXTEEN |

Even after recognizing him, Jemimah still found herself mesmerized. She almost couldn't believe someone could be outstandingly handsome without even making an effort. But the other person had merely glanced at her and said nothing before walking towards the door and opening it.

"Go pick your stuff" It wasn't until after he had spoken that Jemima finally moved from where she was standing. Several questions were running through her mind and Jemima didn't know which one of them to ask first. She gave him a small smile and stepped into the apartment.

Jeremiah had always been a neat freak so she wasn't surprised when the apartment was extremely neat and arranged. She walked past the seating room and headed straight to his bedroom. Four different fancy bags laid by the doorstep and Jemima bent down in one swoop she was already carrying the bags and heading for the door.

Micah chuckled seeing Jemimag holding the bags to herself and with one movement, lifted the bags off her hands and started walking towards the car giving Jemima another view of his back. Jemima didn't think she had stared at anyone she was staring at Micah her entire life. She just couldn't understand how someone could be soooo...

She quickly brought out her phone sending a text to Jeremiaha and asking where he knew and where he had met such a handsome boy. Micah was back in barely two minutes meeting Jemima's eyes.

"Are you done?" he asked and Jemima nodded her head.

"Yes I am" she replied pursuing her lips.

"How do you know my brother?" Jemima asked and Micah turned the lock of the door to meet Jemima's black eyes.

"You should ask your brother. Let's go" Micah replied and Jemima chuckled nodding her head.

"I will. That young man has a lot of explaining to do" Jemima replied walking behind Micah out of the gate. She got into the front seat while Micah got into the driver's seat. Without another word, he had reversed and was already driving out of the street.

"Say something," Jemima said after a while. She had long realized that she just absolutely loved hearing this guy speak, She had no idea who he was but she wanted to hear him speak, she had swooned over the lesser than a few sentences he had spoken. She turned to him watching how his coffee-brown eyes swept over her in one gaze.

"What do you want me to say?" He asked his face still as blank as the first time she had seen him.

"What's your name?" Jemima asked.

"Micah, that's my name" Micah replied and Jemima chuckled.

"We have something in common" Jemima announced proudly while Micah turned to the girl beside him, his lips almost lifting in what someone would call an amused smile.

"What do we have in common?" he asked genuinely curious.

"Our names. Micah is a book in the Bible but it's unusual and you would rarely find someone with that name well you are the first. And my name, Jemima, I had to convince everyone my name was a Biblical name, I didn't even know Job had daughters" Jemima replied and Micah pursed his lips nodding his head.

"See, you agree with me," Jemima said with a proud smile on her lips.

"So you are in what department?" Jemima continued asking.

"Civil Engineering" Micah replied and Jemima was too busy staring at his well-sculptured face to realize that all the guards at the gate had formed one line and standing like they were about to receive the President of the United States as Micah drove in.

"Civil Engineering? You don't look like Civil Engineering Micah, not one bit" Jemima said laughing.

"What do I look like?" Micah asked finding himself curious at whatever came out of Jemima's mouth.

"You look like NUT and D or like International Relations or like Architecture, or like Mathematics" Jemima replied and Micah's brows were pulled upwards questioningly.

"Why would you think I look NUT and D?" Micah asked and Jemima shrugged.

"I don't know but you just do" Jemima replied and furrowed her brows when Micah stopped in front of her hostel.

"How did you know I stay at Queen Elizabeth Hall?" Jemima asked surprised.

"Jeremiah said so" Micah replied and Jemima chuckled nodding her head.

"I should have figured that out" she replied laughing again.

"I don't know if I should say this but you do have a nice face to look at, including your voice," Jemima said winking at Micah before getting down.

She proceeded to open the passenger seat and brought out the fancy bags and peeped through the window of the front seat.

"Thank you, Micah," she said cheerfully and Micah nodded his head watching as Jemima bundled the bags into her arms and started walking into the hostel. He turned to the hostel directly in front of Queen Elizabeth's Hall of Residence and a small smirk formed around his lips. He turned to check if Jemima had stepped into the hostel and immediately reversed the call and his phone rang almost immediately.

His eyes floated over the caller ID and he stretched his left hand to swipe the accept call button.

"King" Black's voice immediately came over the call's radio.

"What is it?" Micah asked pressing down on the accelerator.

"You already know about this don't you?" Black asked, one could easily hear a tinge of tiredness in his voice.

"So?" Micah asked.

"What are you going to do?" Black asked.

"Let them be" Micah replied.

"King!" Black exclaimed.

"I mean it" Micah replied and Black's sigh resounded in his ears.

"What about Hera? She's causing so much trouble. I can't handle her" Black muttered hissing in between his teeth while Micah chuckled.

"Let her be too, her bark has no bite" Micah replied.

"Professor Farida asked of you again" Black informed and Micah furrowed his brows.

"Okay. I'm hungry. Get me something to eat" Micah replied.

"Where are you?" Black asked.

"Leaving school"

"Leaving school? You went to school?" Black asked with surprise in his voice.

"Jemima" Micah replied and there was a minute of silence before Black's voice was heard again.

"So?" Black asked.

"I'm hungry. Get me something to eat"

################

Jemima laughed at Sewa who was typing away on her laptop and Faidat who was shaking her head.

"Will Sewa be able to find him?" Ing asked and Faidat burst into laughter.

"You've been friends with Sewa for this long and you are still unsure whether Sewa would be able to find him on not?" she asked shaking her head.

"Sewa will bring out his IG, Twitter, Snapchat, and phone number very soon. That girl is a social media FBI" she added while Jemima burst into laughter trying to arrange the provisions and necessities her mom had brought.

The moment she had stepped into her room, she had immediately called the girls to tell them about Micah. Sewa wouldn't believe that Micah was the way she had described so they had decided to check if he had any socials.

Vickie had run into her while she was entering the hostel and without a word had helped her with some of the stuff. She dropped them in the room and before Jemima could even say thank you, she had walked out of the room already.

"Found him" Sewa announced and Jemima immediately left her wardrobe and hurried to where her phone was placed.

"His display name sounds even hellass sexy and smart" Sewa continued.

"The O.Micah," she said and Jemima froze. She stared at the screen and realized that it was a name she had seen before. There was only one picture on the Ig account with over 100k followers.

It was Micah and then the name rang a bell in her head.

"Nobody calls him Micah, everyone calls him King. He's the head of the Titans"

"Girls, let me call you back," Jemima said in a rush ending the video call and dialing Jeremiah's number in a rush. The latter picked up at the second ring.

"Jeremiah, I need you to come to my hostel right now," Jemima said her heart shaking with fear and shock.

"Your hostel?" Jeremiah asked shocked.

"What's going on Jemi?" He asked again surprised.

"When the hell were you going to tell me you were a cultist?!" Jemimah yelled into the phone.

"If you don't want me to call Mommy and Daddy right now, come to my hostel" Jemimah added ending the call abruptly while falling to her knees.

She couldn't believe she had found a murderer attractive. Someone who cut off the heads of people and stabbed people, she found him attractive, and she wanted to know more about him. What was she thinking?!

She hugged her knees to herself waiting for Jeremiah to call her back, she desperately hoped that Jeremiah wasn't one of them. That he wasn't a murderer.

Hello guysssss, first I would like to apologize for not replying to the comments under my Birthday post on my conversation page. This is me saying thank you for the gifts, prayers, wishes, and messages. It went a whole long way and I want to say a big thank you to everyone for supporting me as an author even till this very moment. I am saying that "Thank you so so much".

Two is that my birthday gift to y'all came out and you people didn't grab me. Felt me stunned actually. I published a compilation of short stories on Okadabooks titled "SHADES OF YOU" and it cost just Five Hundred Naira only (N500), and as well I'll be running a giveaway for the book on my IG writing page this week and I would be giving two lucky people which has now increased to three lucky people the book for Free.

Third, I'm sorry this update came so lateee, some of y'all have been on my neck likeee. My exams are staring next week Tuesday and I doubt if I'll be able to upload a second chapter before then but a second chapter will surely come this month after my exams because I just have to throw a party. After all, I'll be leaving this level after three years.

NUT and D mean Nutrition and Dietetics. And who else is scared the way I'm scared for Jeremiah and Jemimah? What is she going to do? Man, I'm tenseddd. But then, Micah and Jemima have a huge rapport.

Who else has a social media FBI friend like Sewa or you are the FBI friend?

Keep your fingers crossed for my Giveaway on my IG page.

17 SEVENTEEN

J emima still had her face buried in her lap when Jeremiah called her again. She swallowed as she picked up the call.

"I'm outside your hostel, come out," he said and ended the call. Jemima chuckled angrily getting off her bed and wearing her slippers. Jeremiah had only spent two years at CUA, she desperately prayed that he hadn't killed someone. She almost couldn't believe that Jeremiah was a cultist.

He had always been the coolest of the two of them, he never found trouble even if trouble went looking for him and now upon getting to university, he had joined a cult. And worse a cult that went off with people's heads and they still roamed the school compounds like they had done nothing wrong.

She shivered as she walked towards the main gate of her hostel, she could already make out the image of Jeremiah leaning against a Toyota Camry, something told her that one of the cultists and even worse Micah could own the car.

"Get in" Jeremiah commanded as he started walking towards the driver's seat.

"If this car belongs to any of your cult members or Micah, I'm not getting in" Jemima replied wearing a huge frown.

"If I were you Jemima, I would get into this car right now" Jeremiah shot back and Jemima pulled her head backward.

"Jerry, did you just yell at me?" Jemima asked while Jeremiah pulled his lips into a thin line.

"I won't say it again Jemi, Get into the car," Jeremiah said opening the driver's door and getting into the car. Jemima stared at the tinted window of the car, She couldn't see Jeremiah but she could make out images in her head, him fretting because he didn't know how to explain to her, or the fact that he got caught. If it wasn't Bimbo, Jeremiah never fretted. It wasn't his go-to emotion.

Jemima closed his eyes as Paul and Peter's words rang in her head again. She refused to admit it but she wanted to know that Jeremiah wasn't a part of them. That he wasn't a murderer. Without another thought, she yanked the door open and got it.

"How many people have you killed?" Jemima asked while Jeremiah turned to her with a blank face.

"Jemimah, are you being serious right now?" Jeremiah asked and Jemima sighed softly. Jeremiah's sarcastic reply already answered her question.

"I haven't killed anyone and King isn't who you think he is" Jeremiah added and Jemima turned in her seat to face him.

"I know exactly who he is. He's a murderer!" Jemima yelled the tips of her eyes red.

"And who fed that amount of shit to you Jemima?" Jeremiah asked and Jemima chuckled.

"Doesn't everyone in CUA know this information except me?" Jemima shot back, her reply sending Jeremiah into silence.

"Of every bad and terrible vice you could pick up Jeremiah, you picked up being in a cult? Really?" she asked again and Jeremiah sighed.

"I am not a part of the Titans okay?" Jeremiah replied and Jemima froze.

"You aren't part of the Titans?" she asked her voice unsure.

"I am not a part of the Titans. Why the hell won't you believe me anyway?" Jeremiah asked and Jemimah swallowed resting her back on the seat.

"Then what's your relationship with Micah? He had the keys to your house and hell you have mentioned him a lot of times when talking at home and to Mom and Dad. They wouldn't believe that the King their son always talks about is a murderer and a cultist" Jemima muttered.

"I am very sorry that I can't explain all this to you Jemima because it's not in my place to. But I'll say it again, King isn't who you think he is" Jeremiah replied attempting to defend Micah.

"He killed people Jeremiah; Human beings. Off with their heads just because they didn't want him to be their leader. Nothing ever justifies that Jeremiah" Jemima whispered while Jeremiah's brows pulled backward in a frown.

"Who exactly fed you this shit? I want to know" Jeremiah asked.

"Paul and Peter" Jemima replied and Jeremiah raised an eyebrow.

"Micah didn't kill those guys because they didn't want him to be the leader. He didn't cut off their heads either" Jeremiah replied.

"So you are telling me that Paul and Peter are lying?" Jemima asked chuckling.

"Do you know that you have just defended a murderer? Jeremiah how could you find excuses for him?! She yelled.

"The story that Micah cut off the heads of those guys, only very few people know that story Jemi; only members of the Titans and very, very, very few people know that. I think before you question me over and over again; you should ask your friends where they heard their stories from" Jeremiah replied while Jemima froze.

"What do you mean? Do you mean to say Paul and Petter are cultists? Members of the Titans? Huh?" she asked swallowing.

"Don't try to change the topic Jeremiah" she added and Jeremiah rubbed his forehead.

"Be careful around Heraline" Jeremiah said suddenly while Jemima frowned.

"Excuse you?" she asked and Jeremiah sighed softly.

"Look Jemima, I need you to get your game up, I need you to get your head up and working. Nobody plays friendlies at CUA, not these people. You have to be careful, you can't afford to become a wild card or a chess piece" Jeremiah replied while Jemima folded her arms.

"I absolutely despise it when you talk in parables" Jemimah replied and Jeremiah chuckled.

"I don't have to worry that much because even when I speak in parables, you are smart enough to understand" he added and Jemima swallowed.

"What's going on?" Jemima asked rubbing her glabella.

"You need to be honest and clear with me if you don't want me to turn to a chess piece. Being a wild card seems more promising than that" she added and Jeremiah shook his head.

"Unfortunately, I can't help you with that Jem Jem, you'll have to find out yourself. That way, you'll understand better. Telling you would ruin the show" Jeremiah replied and Jemima squeezed her face.

"I told you not to call me Jem Jem" she retorted and Jeremiah burst into laughter.

"Story for another day but maybe I'll be a late brother to you by now if I hadn't met King" Jeremiah announced and Jemima turned to him in shock.

"Do you mean..." she trailed off and Jeremiah shook his head.

"It's not what you think" he replied and turned to Jemima.

"You remember when people would argue about who was smarter between you and me? When we are back in high school?" Jeremiah asked and Jemima chuckled.

"You still want to show off something so irrelevant?" Jemima asked a small smile on her lips, "You know you only won because the girls liked you more" she added and a smile finally wore its way to Jeremiah's lips.

"I totally agree. You and I know that while I'm way much smarter...." Jeremiah started but got cut short by Jemima.

"Did you really have to say that?" she asked and Jeremiah shrugged.

"I was merely stating a fact Jem Jem" he replied getting back a playful punch from Jemima.

"But you were the best at games, especially Chess, you were good with people, you were perceptive with everyone else and you were that girl Jemima. And I need that girl right now, desperately. I could only have done it on my own because you were in the dark, being ignorant was the best but now that you know, it's only a matter of time before you find out the rest" Jeremiah continued.

"And Jem Jem, you can't trust anyone, nobody at all. It is just me and you" Jeremiah finished and Jemima chuckled.

"You know I absolutely hate this" she revealed and Jeremiah nodded his head with a small smile.

"These are the kind of games you hate the most and also the type of games you are the best at" he replied and Jemima shrugged her shoulders.

"You have to promise me that you reduce your contact with this King guy and the whole cult as a whole. You have to stay away from them" Jemima said pursing her lips.

"I'm afraid I can't" Jeremiah replied and Jemima sighed softly.

"You can't?" she asked and Jeremiah nodded his head.

"Can you then promise me that on no grounds would you ever be a member or ever kill someone no matter what happens?" Jemima asked staring into Jeremiah's brown eyes.

"It's not going to happen Jemima. Ever" he replied and Jemima nodded her head.

"That sounds much better" she replied and a bout of silence ensured between the both of them.

"Jem Jem"

"Huh?"

"You do know that life isn't black or white right?"

"Goodnight Jeremiah. Try not to be a chess piece" Jemima replied opening the door and getting out of the car. She folded her arms and watched Jeremiah drive off. She turned and took a glance at the opposite boys' hostel while walking towards the gate of her hostel.

"Amazing" she whispered into the wind.

The room was already bustling with gossip that went into the air as soon as she stepped into the room. She ignored the looks she was getting from the girls and opened her WhatsApp.

Me: Hey babe, I need your help. 10:37 PM.

Adesewa: You went off the call in a hurry earlier. What's going on? 10:37 PM

Me: When does your Internship start? 10:38 PM

Adesewa: Not until two months' time, I'm planning on going to Nairobi, there's a conference I would like to attend. 10:38 PM

Me: Postpone your trip, I need you to help me find people. 10:39 PM

Adesewa; People? What's going on? 10:39 PM

Me: You need to help me find out. 10:40 PM

Hello everyoneeeeee. I'm so excited to write to you guys again. I will have to keep tendering apologies to you guys every single time I publish a chapter. I am so sorry for keeping you waiting. I saw the emails and the messages, guys, I'm so sorry if I haven't replied to your messages, I won't lie. I don't know if I'll be replying to the messages anytime soon.

I'm currently writing exams and this chapter was written in the middle of my exams. I have two chapters en route this month and I hope that appeases you guys. Thank you so much for your love, time, and support.

Then to business, What the hell is going onnn? You have to be twice as curious as me about what Jeremiah is talking about. Who are these people that don't play friendlies and what do they have to do with Heraline? I honestly want to hear you guys theories.

The best theory gets SHADES OF YOU for free. Hehee, that's attractive, right?

The next chapter also has a surprise, the first person to get the surprise also gets a free copy, and let me give you guys a hint, there's someone you guys have to meet. Hehehe.

And better still, you can head over to Okdabooks and buy the book at 500naira only, support your favourite author with moneyyyyyyyy.

And before you tap on the star button because you are star boys and star girls, don't forget to tag your friends to enjoy this book with you.

Wish me luck in my exams and don't worry. It will be over soon.

xoxo people.

18|EIGHTEEN|

B y the time Jemimah woke up, the room was already half empty with only Ayisat in the room. She was lying on her bed and muttering the lyrics to the song that Jemimah was sure she had heard before so she didn't even bother to try to think about it.

Taking her bath and dressing up which normally took a few minutes took Jemima up to an hour. Her eyes were unfocused and her mind was in disarray. Her discussion with Jeremiah the previous night had pointed out a lot of things she had previously ignored and didn't read meanings to. She grabbed her edge control and lipgloss in her wardrobe before turning towards the general restrooms. While each room had a bathroom and toilet, there were still general restrooms at the end of each floor with long full-length mirrors that allowed the girls to take multiple and millions of mirror selfies and pictures.

But the moment Jemimah stepped into the general restroom, she felt her mind go blank at the sight of the person in front of her. Even her unarranged thoughts seemed to have placed themselves on hold while she stared at the person in front of her.

"I'm sure you heard something along the lines of it's not polite to stare at someone and especially so blatantly," the girl said and Jemimah snapped out of her reverie before walking towards the mirror and placing her edge control on the basin.

Jemimah's eyes met the other girl's eyes in the mirror and she watched as the girl turned to her.

'Wow, you are really pretty" she exclaimed with surprise written all over her face while Jemima merely smiled.

"Thank you Annabelle" she replied. Getting such a compliment from someone like Annabelle was top tier but Jemimah had heard the same thing almost every day of her life, she wasn't going to start squealing and blushing like some two-year-old given candy.

"Are you a model?' Annabelle asked turning to the girl beside her while Jemimah shook her head.

"No, I'm not" Jemima replied.

"That's shocking. That they let someone with your face roam about without standing on your neck" Annabelle commented and Jemimah shrugged.

"Of course, they didn't. I'm not just so cut out for that kind of life so I turned it down, turned down a lot" Jemimah replied and Annabelle nodded her head.

"You are quite very self-aware" she added a small smile gracing her lips.

"What's your name?" she asked.

"Jemimah. Adeleke Jemimah" Jemimah replied turning to the taller girl.

"I thought you stayed outside school" Jemimah commented and Annabelle rolled her eyes.

"My manager thought it was a good idea to mingle" Annabelle replied emphasizing the mingle and saying it in a way that made Jemimah burst into laughter. She could see why despite her arrogant nature, people loved her. She was actually relaxing to be around and it surprised Jemimah.

"You do need to mingle" Jemimah replied and Annabelle chuckled lightly, an amused smile on her lips.

"You know what Jemi? I have this shoot soon and we need a dark-skinned model. I don't know if you would want to fill in" Annabelle said and Jemimah stared at her without words.

Whatever shoot Annabelle was talking about, Jemimah knew it wasn't a small-scale shoot. The fact that Annabelle was asking her was even more of a shock.

"You don't have to think so much, it's your choice" Annabelle chipped in and Jemimah chuckled.

"Yeah. I'll love too" Jemimah replied and Annabelle immediately whipped out her phone stretching it out toward Jemimah.

"Save your contact" she replied and Jemimah smiled collecting the phone and pressing her digits and saving it.

"I have a class in a few minutes so have a great day" Annabelle added and Jemimah nodded her head.

"Sure, sure, sure" Jemimah replied.

"Please don't forget to mingle," Jemimah said as Annabelle started walking out of the restroom. The reply she got an amused smile at the corner of Annabelle's lips and an eye roll. Jemimah had a lot of celebrity friends, Farida was one of the most popular royal figures in the country and was even gaining a lot of recognition in the world among others, adding Annabelle to the list gave some sort of excitement to Jemimah. She knew she was different.

"She's actually a sweet person", "Amazing".

18+ CONTENT

"Do you have the timer ready?" the girl asked while the latter nodded her head, her eyes fixed on the exquisite body in front of her.

The girl in front of her was clad in the usual swimming attire, molding her lean and slim body. Her long legs graced the upper part of her body and the girl watched as she strode towards the swimming area, wearing her goggles over her eyes.

"Go" she shouted and the girl jumped into the water swimming with all her strength, she glanced from the girl to the stopwatch in her hands a huge smile on her face.

Within seconds, the girl's head had emerged from the water and she removed her goggles from her eyes.

"Time?" she asked.

"One minute, seventeen seconds" she replied folding her arms and shaking her head.

"You broke your record again" she added while the girl snickered.

"I want to at least be done in fifteen seconds" she muttered getting out of water while the latter chuckled.

"Niyi, you know that this is huge already. Before you couldn't even pass the twenty seconds benchmark no matter what and now you've beaten it" she replied hoping to console her.

"Well I need to hit that fifteen-second benchmark if I am to beat that genius swimmer" Niyi replied venom in her words and the other girl swallowed.

"You are going to beat her if you keep this up" the girl replied again and Niyi chuckled.

"Thank you very much, Amara," Niyi said an amused smile on her lips but Amara knew better. She knew that Niyi was just being sarcastic. She watched as Niyi wrapped her towel around her.

"Are you going to Charles's house party?" Amara asked carefully and Niyi rolled her eyes.

"Why?" Niyi asked, "You want to tag along?" she asked but before Amara could reply, another voice interrupted them.

"Hello girlssss" a masculine voice rang in the air and both girls turned.

"Charles?" Amara called out in surprise.

"Hi Amara" Charles replied closing the distance between them and pressing a kiss to her cheeks freezing Amara in place.

"Oh my baby" Charles cooed moving towards Niyi and enveloping her in a hug.

"I knew I was going to find you here" Charles muttered leaving his hands around Niyi's waist while the latter wore a sleazy smile and wrapped her hands around his neck.

"You haven't even spoken to me since this semester started. Why are you looking for me?' Niyi asked and Charles smiled.

"It's of course to invite you to my house party. I'm sure you know about it. I came specially to invite you" Charles replied and Niyi chuckled.

"Specially?" she asked and Charles nodded his head closing the already small distance between them and placing his lips on hers. Niyi didn't shy away from the kiss choosing to actively participate. She arched her head meeting Charles's lips in a more convenient position while sucking on his lips with so much concentration, her tongue slid inside Charles's mouth exploring and licking every wall inside his mouth, their tongues interwove and Niyi moaned lightly feeling Charles licking the walls of her mouth and even attempting to give her a deep throat kiss. Despite being unable to breathe properly, neither of the two gave leeway and continued kissing like their lives depended on it.

Charles let one of his hands leave her waist and moved towards the towel she was wrapping around her body. With a small tug, the towel came apart revealing her gorgeous body. His fingers were quick to find the buckle of her swimming trunk and Niyi gasped opening her eyes and finding Amara still standing by the side, frozen with her fingers clenched and biting into her palms. A sleazy smile appeared on her lips and she chuckled quietly.

"Let me" she whispered to Charles pulling the entire swimming trunk over her head, leaving her bare naked body. Charles didn't think twice about rushing towards her breasts, cupping and massaging one of them while sucking on the other. Niyi threw her head back moaning and running her hands through his hair.

The both of them had long forgotten that there was a human being standing right beside them watching them. Charles moved his onslaught to the next nippled sucking with reckless abandon that made Amara's ears fill with Niyi's moans but neither could she move a muscle nor could she block her ears from hearing it.

"Amara you are not going to leave?" Niyi suddenly asked pausing Charles's movement as he turned to face Amara. A surprised look spread across his face and Amara gulped.

"You didn't leave?" he asked turning to Niyi with an amused expression.

"She didn't leave since the beginning?" he asked and Niyi smiled nodding her head.

"Nope"

"Why didn't you say anything?" he asked unhappily and Niyi burst into laughter.

"At least I told you before you went any further" she replied a smile crawling up her lips. She bent down and picked up the towel wrapping it around her body.

"I'll be there. I'll be at your party" Niyi announced and Charles grinned.

"See you then" he replied turning to Amara.

"Sorry, you had to witness that. Will you come to the party with Niyi?" Charles asked and Amara immediately shook her head.

"I have some undone assignments, so I won't be able to make it" Amara replied and Charles nodded his head.

"Oops, that's sad. See you" he muttered before walking away.

Amara's head was dropped down, her fingers still biting into her palms. The way they kissed, the way they held each other, she needed nobody to tell her it wasn't their first time, they had gotten together enough times to get used to each other like that. Niyi calling Charles's attention to the fact that she was present didn't help matters either. She couldn't help but notice that Charles's unhappiness had to do with the fact that she didn't leave not the fact that he was embarrassed.

"You suddenly have assignments?" Niyi asked and Amara raised her head up nodding.

"Weren't you asking me right before Charles came if I was going to the party?" Niyi asked an amused smile on her lips.

"Or is it because of what you saw?" she asked again and Amara swallowed her saliva. Meeting the other girl's eyes, she knew that she had done it intentionally. She knew what she doing, she was so wrong, she had been so so wrong that she could trust her or even be friends with her.

"I'm leaving Niyi" Amara muttered dropping the stopwatch and turning to leave.

"He doesn't like you. People like you" Niyi said suddenly bringing a stop to Amara's movement.

"You saw" Niyi added folding her arms and Amara turned to her with a small chuckle on her lips.

"This is why everyone stays away from you" Amara muttered willingly herself not to let a single tear fall.

"I know that you are capable of having anyone you want Niyioluwa, anyone at all, you can fuck whoever you want but I promise you, you will be alone till you die" Amara added with an eerie calm before turning and finally walking away.

Niyi shook her head "She's so petty"

I promised a certain someone to write another chapter before this month ends and phew, here's the next chapter before the month ends. Much to my disappointment, you people refuse to comment on the last chapter even though I had dropped juicy offers. Are you guys that angry with me?

Please, guys, let go of your anger, I'm a student with a department that threatens to take my life every two market days, every day in fact so please bear with me. It's going to actually get better guys so Biane, I'm sorry.

What's your opinion about Niyioluwa? She's very mad in my opinion. Very mad.

And the kissing scene was just gross. Stills feels weird dang. But I hope you enjoyed it anyway. We are about to get right into the drama so stay glued and tag every one you know, every single person you think would love this book.

And Happy New Month in advance everybody. Don't forget to follow me on Instagram (_the.girlsemi) in case you don't.

Love, SEMILOORE.

19 NINETEEN

I MPORTANT ANNOUCEMENT - There's a piece of important information in my Author's note below this chapter, don't miss it. Don't say I didn't tell you. (winks winks)

SUG member B who specializes in disseminating information within the school has been accused of sexual assault and sexual harassment. B had taken a liking to a girl E in another department and had been chasing her for a very long time and yet has always been turned down by E who felt like he was not her style but B yet chasing E effortlessly.

After successfully dragging her to a party with him, B drugged her drink and then molested and assaulted her. When E woke up and questioned B, he denied all charges leveled against him.

Jemima chuckled dropping her phone and turning to her friends, "Who the hell is this Butterfly Fairy?" she asked displeasure written all over her face.

"You are angry at her for revealing such information," Paul asked narrowing his eyes while Peter scoffed.

"You should be angry at B for molesting another woman not angry at ButterFly Fairy for revealing the news" He added.

"ButterFly Fairy disgusts me on a normal day but today, I agree with her" Doyin chipped in and Jemimah scoffed again.

"You are right, this post is just another piece of evidence to show that ButterFly Fairy is a woman. And a thoughtless woman at that" Jemima replied.

"What makes you say so? This person is a SUG member, the school might not even allow her to report him to the police and he might just get away with the suspension of one semester, and trust me, he'll be allowed to come and write his tests and exams" Peter informed and Jemima nodded her head.

"SUG member B who specialises in disseminating information within the school already gave whatever information she was trying to hide away. She's talking about the Public Relations Officer and who doesn't know him?" Jemimah asked.

"You think everyone is stupid? It's easy to ask around what girl he had been hanging around with and what parties he had attended recently. And people talk, CUA students majorly love to do the talking, I bet someone has the girl's information on the forum already" Jemima continued.

"If this girl had in reality confided in ButterFly Fairy to tell her, her story then ButterFly Fairy is an idiot. She has successfully given the girl away, it's a matter of time before they find her, and if the SUG is as powerful as you say, it will soon be debunked as false news. You'll see the girl coming out herself to deny all charges leveled against him" Jemimah finished while the trio stared at her in surprise and awe.

"I honestly didn't think that far" Paul muttered nodding his head.

"I mean that's some rational thinking there" Doyin added.

"You are always so rational, I can't wait to see you flustered and all over the place" Peter announced while Paul burst into laughter.

"Flustered? All over the place?" Jemima asked and Peter nodded his head.

"You are not going to see it" Jemima replied with an amused expression on her face.

"Why?" Peter asked and Jemima just shrugged.

"Situations and circumstances that put me in states like that, I avoid it" Jemima replied as Peter's smile got wider.

"What if you can't avoid such a situation?" Peter asked and Jemimah burst into laughter.

"I hate to boast. But who am I? If I want to, I'll avoid it" Jemima replied.

"Your confidence is amazing Jemi," Paul said and Jemimah laughed.

"That's the first time you are calling me that" she revealed and Paul smiled.

"Enough with your flustered confidence conversation, can we go to the hostel now?" Doyin asked.

"I'm famished" she added as Peter stretched one of his hands to rub her head while the other hand grabbed Jemima's bag.

"When you get hungry, English words aside the term food becomes a foreign word to you," Peter said and they burst into laughter.

"Don't make fun of me okay?" Doyin cooed as they walked out of the Lecture theater.

Jemima turned to Doyin as she scrolled through her phone, "I only made a guess, and the forums crawling with blog posts about who she is. Some third-year student of Accounting" Jemima said shaking her head.

"That's Abraham's department isn't it?" she asked no one in particular as she slipped her phone into her pocket.

"I have no words for this ButterFly Fairy girl, she has just successfully landed her in trouble" Doyin joined in the conversation while Jemima folded her arms.

"Trouble is an understatement. Even if the school decides to treat this properly; she will forever get that kind of look. The 'that was the girl that got sexually assaulted', 'oh my God, I pity her so much', and 'I heard she got pregnant and aborted the baby'. Those kinds of looks and words won't be so far from her" Jemima added while Doyin shook her head.

"I don't know what to say. In a bid to help her, she has landed her in trouble and put her in a mess. Even if the girl comes out and says it's a lie, the stigma would still be there, people would still whisper and people would come up with all kinds of conjectures" Doyin added.

"And worse, it's irritating me that this mess could have been solved if only the person took her English classes well," Jemima said turning the doorknob of her room and stepping into the room. The other three girls were already in the room and they were all staring at the duo that had just entered as though they had been waiting for them.

"Where have you been?" Vickie asked folding her arms while Jemima stared at her weirdly. Alarms bells had gone off in her head the moment she walked into the room, the way the girls had been staring at her was another, Vickie standing in front of her with folded arms and irritated eyes was another sign.

"Is there a problem?" Doyin asked.

"Care to explain where you got this biscuit?" Vickie asked revealing the satchet of the biscuit she had eaten the night before. Vickie also had the same brand of biscuit seating in her wardrobe. Jemima dropped her head and laughed quietly raising her head and meeting Vickie's hard gaze in the middle. Irritation flashed through her ears as she kept up the staring competition with Vickie.

"I sincerely hope that it's not what I'm thinking," Jemima said slowly while Vickie threw the nylon to the floor.

"I am the only one who has this biscuit in this room, I haven't eaten any in the past few days, what is a nylon doing on the floor of the room?" Vickie shot at Jemima.

"You took advantage of me when my wardrobe was open right? That's when you took it" Vickie continued shaking her head.

"I do know that we aren't on good terms but I wouldn't think twice if you asked me. I would have given you gladly" Vickie said snickering.

"But you had to steal it"

"Shut up!" Jemima said rather calmly while Vickie stared at her in surprise dumbfounded.

'Excuse me?" she croaked out in shock.

"Are you talking to me?" she asked pointing to herself.

"Who else? Do you think I'm trying to converse with your dead grandmother here?" Jemima shot back a small smile on her lips.

"Steal? Why would I steal from you when there are two packs of the biscuit sitting down in my wardrobe?!" Jemima yelled and everyone shrunk in both shock and surprise.

"Jemima you need to calm down," Doyin said trying to appease her.

'Don't think too highly of yourself Vickie, you aren't that high" Jemima continued walking towards her wardrobe and opening it. She bent to the lowest compartment and in two moves, two packs of the biscuits were lying on the floor of the room leaving them in shock.

"Didn't Vickie say her father sent it from Paris?" Ayisat asked.

"Isn't that she's so angry?" Tamiloore whispered back.

"How the hell does Jemima have two packs?' Ayisat whispered back rather very loudly.

"One warning Vickie that should never repeat itself, don't ever accuse me of something I have no idea or have never done before, don't fold your arms in front of me and stand like you are God Almighty, you aren't. Stop thinking the world revolves around you, heck you aren't even a President's daughter, so why do you keep acting like the world is revolving around you?" Jemima shot question after question at Vickie who just stood there unable to form words together.

"Ask you? I'd rather not have it than take anything from you. You are too lousy" Jemima finished bending down and returning the boxes to their usual position.

"You didn't think to accuse your friends Ayisat and Tamiloore who are always all over your wardrobe and your bed but you chose to accuse me. How amazing" Jemima started again dropping her bad on her bed.

"That's enough, I'm sure she just got confused for a moment," Doyin said trying to ease the tense atmosphere in the room.

"I'm sorry"

Have I told y'all HAPPY NEW MONTH yet? If I have or if I haven't, HAPPY NEW MONTH my people. I pray that this new month brings clarity and good tidings. If your birthday is in October, feel free to send me a DM and get a chapter dedicated to you.

At this point, ButterFly Fairy is getting more mysterious to me. Who the hell are you? And I'm more amazed that someone even dared to confide in her but what can I say? Who knows what would happen next?

And I have no words for Vickie at this point, she accused our woman of stealing, stealing biscuits o, not money or even something huge. Loved how Jemima put her back in her place. Will Jemima and her roommates ever get a rommie relationship? At this point, I can't even dare to guess because these ones ehn.

Comment you thoughts if Jemima and her roommates will ever have a roomie relationship. I think they won't. Ugh, they are annoying.

NOW TO THE BIGGEST NEWS OF THE MONTHHHHHHH-HHHHH.

For the longest time, I've had people always asking me, do you have a reader fna group where your fans can talk about your book and relate with you and the answer has always been no but as of this moment, the answer is a yessss. If you are an avid reader of my books, please fly or teleport to my Instagram page (_the.girlsemi) and link on the whatsapp link in my bio to join the group asap. There are lot of juicy things available on the group and Imean you also get to relate with me and me with you guysss. I'm so excited and I hope y'all are too.

This isn't a solid promise but updates are going to regular this month, maybe 'extra' regular infact. Don't forget to tap on the Star button at the end of this chapter and yesss.

Tag Festttt - Tag your friends to come check out this amazing book.

Love, from who else? Me of course.

20 TWENTY

Dedicated to Happy Birthday Sweetie. The Lord is your portion in this new year, you find clarity and whatever you lay your hands upon prospers. Have a great year ahead!

Jemima chuckled after following Doyin back to her room. She was stunned that Vickie had apologized with a few words and worse Jemima knew her apology was sincere and honest, it honestly irked her even more.

But Vickie accusing her of stealing her biscuits blew her over the top. Biscuits? Biscuits? Danish-made biscuits?

Jemima could only drop her head and laugh at the thought. She couldn't imagine what kind of image she had in Vickie's mind for her to have been accused of stealing biscuits when there were hundreds more attractive things in her wardrobe.

As she walked closer to her room, she could hear voices since the room door was slightly ajar and she immediately rolled her eyes. Something told her the girls were gossiping about her; so instead of walking directly into the room, she leaned by the doorside listening to their conversation.

"I told you it was a bad idea," Vickie said her brows pulled in a frown.

"What else did you want to do?' Ayisat asked.

"But do you think they are dating?" Vickie asked again uncertainty and nervousness in her voice and Jemima pulled her brows together.

Who was she dating now?

"He was carrying her bag the last time and he was carrying her bag as well today. I think that answers your questions" Tamiloore replied and Jemima stared at the door an amused smile crawling up her face.

"I didn't know Peter liked girls like Jemima," Ayisat said and Jemima frowned, her smile wiping off immediately but she was soon stunned into shock.

"What's wrong with Jemima?' Vickie asked suddenly.

"Girls like Jemima?" she asked again chuckling.

"C'mon Ayisat, I know you are jealous because Jemima is bougie as hell. She's classy and just that girl you want to be friends with but at the same time can't be because you don't know what she thinks of you" Vickie added.

"Aren't you speaking too highly of her Vickie? I thought you didn't like her" Tamiloore said and Vickie turned to her wordlessly.

"Me? Did I ever say I didn't like her?" she asked and Tamiloore stared at her mouth agape.

"Stop pretending guys, you are jealous of her. Every one of us" Vickie revealed.

"I'm not jealous of her" Ayisat defended.

"Me too. I have nothing to be jealous of" Tamiloore chipped in and Vickie chuckled.

"I saw you looking at her Instagram and Twitter page. Four times I think" Vickie shot back and Ayisat chuckled.

"And you Tamiloore, I know you have separate accounts that follow all her socials. She has only one video on Tiktok but you've watched it like a hundred times because you can't get over how good her outfit looked" Vickie added looking to and from between the two girls.

"You can't lie to me, okay?" she said raising her hands upwards.

"Okay! Satisfied that you've exposed me now?" she asked and Vickie sighed sitting down on her bed.

"I'm not a stalker" Tamiloore grumbled and Vickie rolled her eyes.

"That's the least of my problems. If Peter likes Jemima, I have zero chances with him okay?" Vickie said and Jemima pushed the door slightly and walked into the rooms.

She watched as Vickie grabbed her iPad from her bag and climbed into her bed scrolling through whatever without another word.

If someone had told Jemima Vickie had said those words, she wouldn't have believed it. She wouldn't have believed either that her roommates actually had such opinions of her.

They always acted as though they didn't like her and left her out of their conversations like they didn't want to converse with her.

They had been scared she would have told them off. Jemima couldn't wrap her head around it. Leaving the door slightly open had given Jemima information that she was sure that even if they were at gunpoint, the girls wouldn't have admitted.

She took another glance at them and shook her head, they were superb pretenders, way too good pretenders. They would pass as amazing actresses all of them, especially Vickie. Her brows pulled her questioningly as she stole another glance at the girl staring at her iPad across her.

She was so focused on what she was doing that nothing in the room seemed to be able to hold her attention.

How had she managed to notice things about Ayisat and Tamiloore that even she herself hadn't noticed? She had an amazing keen ability and Jemima couldn't help but admire it. Remembering why she had picked up a fight with her in the first place, she burst into laughter drawing everyone's attention in the room.

"Sorry guys" Jemima apologized shaking her head.

Vickie had picked a fight with her because of Peter?

The thought made Jemima want to burst into laughter again but she didn't want to be treated as a senile person even if it was for a few seconds. She was so going to tell Peter and Paul and see their reaction and what they had to say. Doyin would be mortified at the turn of events.

——--"I have something really funny to tell you guys" Jemima started crossing her legs underneath her with an amused smile.

"Let me fill you guys in," Doyin said excitedly.

"Jemi's roommates accused her of stealing biscuits yesterday" Doyin started and both Paul and Peter burst into laughter simultaneously.

"Biscuits? You mean literal biscuit" Paul said and Doyin nodded her head.

"It wasn't as funny as this yesterday' she replied and Peter chuckled.

"Your roommates are nuts" he commented and Doyin burst into laughter.

"You need to have seen their faces when Jemi pulled out two cartoons of the same biscuit from her wardrobe. The slap was so satisfying" Doyin continued and they burst into laughter again."But that's really rude" Paul added shaking his head.

"I mean you aren't a two-year-old to be accused of stealing biscuits" Paul continued and Jemima laughed.

"After I followed Doyin back to her room and came back right, I overheard them discussing" Jemima started turning to Peter and shaking her head.

"You wouldn't believe why they had picked a fight with me," Jemima said.

"They had a reason?" Doyin asked in surprise.

"Yes. Vickie sure did" Jemima replied laughing turning to Peter and staring at him as if trying to imprint his face to memory.

"Peter" she announced.

"What does Peter have to do with Vickie accusing you of stealing her biscuit?" Doyin asked confused.

"Well Vickie has a crush on Peter and she apparently saw him carrying my bag for me twice. She concluded that we were dating and boom, I deserve to be punished for dating her crush" Jemima replied and Paul burst into laughter while an amused smile crawled up Peter's lips.

"Vickie has a crush on Peter?" Doyin asked chuckling.

"I mean, they picked a fight with me because of you," Jemima said stretching her pulling Peter's cheeks. She had never really taken notice of Peter's features before, since they bonded quite easily, her brain had registered him as a friend and so she never really took time to look at him before.

Paul and Peter were mirrors of each other yet they were different. They were both handsome and cute and had charming features of themselves. Peter's charm was enough to make a woman swoon, his smiles could send you into fits of delusion and you wouldn't even know or realize it. He was a guy girls would definitely chase after but he just didn't in any way appeal to her.

"Is she pretty?" Peter asked and Jemima burst into laughter.

"Oh yeah. She is" Jemima replied still laughing.

"She's pretty but she's the nastiest soul you'll ever meet. She's petty too. Likes to think she is the daughter of the President and so she's above everyone else. She likes to treat the other two as though they are her slaves" Doyin added nonchalantly.

"Safe to say the only good thing about her is her fine face. I'm sure you don't want her around you" she continued.

"I don't like her one bit. I don't think you are going to like her one-bit" Doyin finished and Peter nodded his head.

"Give her my number Jemi," he said chuckling and Doyin stared at him dazed. She quietly stood up and walked out of the lecture theater. Paul crossed his legs and watched the exiting girl with a blank face.

"Doyin! Where are you going?!" Jemima hollered but Doyin didn't even turn to reply or answer her. Jemima looked on weirdly and turned to the two boys beside her.

"What happened just now?" she asked

"Did she not hear me?" she asked and Paul shook his head with a sleazy smile.

"Nope. She definitely heard you" Paul replied and Jemima tilted her head trying to recount what had just happened and if she had said anything wrong but nothing occurred to her.

"Just give her some minutes," Peter said turning his head to meet Paul's cold gaze but smiling mouth.

"Yeah. I agree with Peter, give her a few minutes" Paul chipped in turning his face to Jemima.

"So do you mean it? You asked me to give Vickie your number?" Jemima asked and Peter nodded his head.

"Yeah. Give it to her"

Hello guys, I deeply apologize for the lack of update last week. I'm going to try to make it up to you guys by trying to update twice or maybe thrice this week. The drama is finally starting and I can't wait to dive innn. I think this is the point where you visit my Instagram page again and watch both the character introduction videos and the trailer itself. And again, if you've not joined StarHouse, you are wronggggg. (_the.girlsemi) is my username on Insta; click on the link in my bio and join StarHouse asap! If you will be active though.

Jemima can't be alone in her mortification of what she heard from her roommates. These girls are amazing actresses. I totally agree with Jemima sha. I used to have that same notion they had about someone and guess what? We are so close now and all that cold exterior that used to send me running feels like a joke now.

P.S: winks twice - who saw what I saw? Well, if you saw it, hmmm, if you didn't nawa o.

21 'TWENTY - ONE'

This chapter is dedicated to , we had our first GAMES NIGHT and she won. You should really join The StarHouse if you haven't.

Micah sat down his legs treched to the front while his eyes remained closed, the whole seating room was dead silent while three guys including Black stood to the side, uncertainty on their faces. Queen also sat down on another chair with the same uncertainty on her face. She raised her head and caught Black's gaze who shook his head at her.

King was angry. He especially hated when they did something messy especially after he had told them to be careful with it. One of the boys finally opened his mouth shakingly.

"King I swear, we took care of it quietly. Nobody knew, even Akin knew nothing about it. As for how this ButterFly Fairy person knew about it, we have no idea" the guy spoke up his lips quivering. His outburst was meant with the same silence as when they had first entered. His hands were clenched to the sides with fury in his heart towards whoever this ButterFly Fiary was.

"King" Black called and Micah finally opened his eyes slowly. He slowly turned to Black, his cold gaze sending black into a three-second fright.

"You want to take responsibility?" he asked and Black visibly gulped before nodding his head.

"They were careful. Something went wrong with the girl. We interrogated Akande but he was certain that nobody else apart from us knew what was going on" Black replied.

"The girl disappeared from school yesterday. ButterFly Fairy's post has put the school in a dilemma, they can't let go of the matter so easily" he added and Micah smirked.

"They will let go" he commented airly with confidence as he retracted his legs and sat down comfortably on the chair.

"And have you found this ButterFly Fairy girl?" Micah asked and Queen finally opened her mouth as well.

"She was surprisingly careful. Whoever she is, the student ID used to open that account belongs to someone who went for an exchange in Turkey. I don't know how the student ID is active. I sent a message to the owner of the student ID, she claimed she gave no one her account and sent over details of people who could have it. Two of them are girls, and three of them are boys. We've checked the boys, they are clean and the girls as well, one of them is in the final year, and the other is also in her fourth year, she isn't the one" Queen explained while Micah's face remained unmoving.

"And?" he asked and Queen swallowed meeting Black's gaze midway again. These days, King was getting more irritable and if she sent one wrong word, she was going to be dead.

"She needs to make one more post and I'll find her" She declared and Micah scoffed.

"One more post? Do I look like I have time for that?" he asked and Queen shook her head quietly.

"Give Seth a call, I want to know whoever dared to mess with me before nightfall" Micah commanded and the two boys nodded their heads bowing their heads slightly before sprinting out of the room.

"What are we going to do about Akande? He asked for protection, that's why he came to us in the first place" Black asked and Micah rubbed his glabella.

"The Ravens are really getting on my nerves these days, I'm beginning to get annoyed" Micah replied, a small frown decorating his brows. His hands went to his pocket and he sighed seeing it was empty.

"Get me a pack of cigarettes from the cupboard or check the table in my room," Micah said as Black nodded his head and walked away.

"You know that Professor Farida has been asking for you consistently, she wouldn't even back off" Queen informed Micah, a huge frown on her face. She was more than irritated. If someone told her a Professor would be such a pest, she wouldn't have believed it but it was right in her front. Each time she ran into anyone who she knew was affiliated with Micah, she would ask about it. She had even intentionally gone to Black's Faculty to wait for him and ask about Micah.

"She's been a pest" Queen added her nose flaring.

"Who decides that she's a pest?" Micah asked coldly and Queen went numb lowering her head.

"My apologies King" she muttered her fingers digging into her skin.

Micah was intentionally accommodating Professor Farida's pestering. No matter how many times she asked to see him, he hadn't gone to see her and had even blocked her number cutting contact with him. She would have thought that he had a thing for her if she didn't know Professor Fairda's position.

That witch

She muttered underneath her breadth. It had taken just one night for her to fall head over heels for Micah. She wasn't surprised considering Micah's charm but she was much older and should even try to play another card instead of pestering Micah like a child who got her candy taken away from her.

"I'll take care of Professor's Farida business myself. I don't need you to remind me what and whatnot is going on" Micah added and Queen kept her head bent his fingers digging harder into her palm.

"Yes King" she replied. She was going to teach that bitch a lesson by herself.

Black stepped outside Micah's room with a blank expression while pursing his lips "Err, King, someone you've exhausted your cigarettes" Black announced and Micah looked at him surprised.

"Like every single one? There's no single cigarette in this whole house?" Micah asked in mockery and Black swallowed.

"Your mint jar is empty too" he added and Micah scoffed.

"How....." Micah started but paused midway rubbing his forehead. He had wanted to ask why no one had restocked his cigarettes or mints but the last time someone had, they had gotten the wrong brand and so he had angrily told them not to get him anything and he was going to get them by himself.

He was getting more and more irritable these days and he knew it. Even the boys were getting careful around them, nobody wanted to be a scapegoat. He liked to plan meticulously and loved it whenever things went according to the plan, he hated flaws and inconsistencies and even hated it more when he did something careful and his plans ended up getting thwarted.

"Let's go get some" Micah finally spoke and Black nodded his head, grabbed a car key from the table, and walked after Micah out of the house. They got into the car and Micah pushed his chair backward closing his eyes again as Black reversed out of the compound.

"King" Black called after a while.

"Hmmm," King responded airly.

"What are you going to do about Professor Farida, she's starting..." Black paused middway speaking shaking his head as if unsure of what to say.

"Starting to what?" Micah asked.

"Starting to be a nuisance. She goes over to some of our boys' Faculties and starts asking about him. She came to my Faculty yesterday, and waited till I finished class" Black replied irritated. A small smile spread across Micah's lips.

"She wants me to fuck her that much?" he asked and Black almost burst into laughter.

"We've drawn her in enough. I think you need to see her to get her off everyone's back for now" Black replied and Micah chuckled again.

"Hmmm" I've heard you" he replied and Black sighed softly as he continued driving. They soon got to their usual supermarket and Black parked in the car park and they both got down from the car. Black took the lead in walking into the supermarket. It was not as full as Black thought it was going to be and grabbed a trolley ignoring the stares that came their way.

Micah merely glanced at the group of people huddled together whispering and in one second, they had scurried away. He slipped his hands into his pockets allowing Black to push the trolley around till they got to the cigarattes section. Black glanced at the attendant who instantly jumped to his feet upon seeing them.

"Good evening King" he greeted gulping.

"Twenty packs," Black said and the attendant gulped nodding his head, opening the door behind him, and started bringing out packs of cigarettes while Black transported them into the trolley. Soon the trolley was half full and Black nodded at the attendant.

"Thank you" he muttered pushing the trolley towards the snacks and chocolates section. Micah stretched his hand and attempted to tear one of the packs open and Black turned to him with a questioning stare.

"You forgot" Black stated.

"No smoking on the premises" he added and Micah almost did an eye roll before slipping his hand back into his pocket without saying anything. He was too irritated and wanted a smoke, hoping to calm his frayed nerves.

A smile wore its way to Black's face as soon as a face came into view "Jemima, is that you?" Black asked and the girl picking chocolates paused and turned to the two of them. Black furrowed his brows as he watched the girl stare at them vigilantly. There was fear in her eyes and she looked unwelcoming. He turned behind him to see Micah staring at her and she at him. He chuckled quietly.

She finally found out? Who told her?

"Are you also...." Jemima finally replied stuttering and pausing midway.

"Are you also... Are you also..." Jemima kept stuttering unable to finish a sentence.

"Do you want to ask if I'm a part of the Titans?" Black asked straightforwardly and Jemima immediately nodded her head.

"Yes, I am"

Hello guysssss. Hehehe, Jemima had known the truth now, She knows who Black is, she knows who Micah is, Who can guess what her next line of action is going to be.

Besides, what were the chances of them running into each other in the supermarket? I don't know but well, we'll see. I had a chapter goal for this month and hopefully, I'll be able to reach it.

And again, Don't forget to visit my Instagram page to join The StarHouse and meet your fellow fans.

Don't forget to spam with votes and comments. Let's hear your thoughtsss.

22 TWENTY-TWO

This chapter is dedicated to Thank you, everyone, for the 8k reads, let's do more. Love you guys.

"My cookies and Chocolates are almost done," Jemima said as Doyin nodded her head munching on her piece of chocolate. Ever since she barged out of the lecture theater the day before, Doyin had been acting out of sorts and rather weirdly. Jemima had chosen not to ask what was going on. She was also giving the twins the silent treatment.

She had not said a word to Paul or Peter throughout that day. It made Jemima worried and at the same time made her feel on edge, like there was something she didn't she didn't know.

"Should we go get some outside?" Doyin offered surprising Jemima who blinked her big eyes at her.

"You want to go out?" she asked and Doyin nodded her head. "Don't you?" she asked and Jemima laughed, her voice flat.

"Considering how you've been acting these days, I didn't think you would want to go out" Jemima replied and Doyin froze for a few seconds as she sat on Jemima's bed.

"Look. Jemi, I'm really sorry about today and yesterday. I'm irritated of some sort and I can't figure it out" Doyin replied, and Jemima slowly nodded.

"Do you want to talk about it?" she asked and Doyin shook her head.

"I think that would even put me in a more irritatable state" She revealed.

"Let's go to the supermarket, there are some other things I'd like to get," Jemima said walking towards her wardrobe and replacing her crop top with a large round neck.

"Do you need to change?"Jemima asked and the latter shook her head.

"Then let's go"

Jemima locked the door behind her and dropped the key at the usual place, walking out of the hostel with Doyin with her eyes squinted. She genuinely hated whatever was going on between Doyin and everyone else. She had played the scene in her head a hundred times and had yet to find something that could have set off Doyin.

The boys had tried to talk to her earlier that day and Doyin had treated them like they didn't exist, while it had made Peter withdraw, Paul was rather undisturbed. He had even assured her not to worry that Doyin would come around soon. Made her suddenly feel displaced out of their friendship, maybe it was something Peter and Paul were used to from their long years of friendship.

If Adesewa, Farida, or Ing would have gotten into such moods; they would have it taken care of already. She genuinely missed her friends. The trip to the supermarket was a rather very silent one. Both girls were focused on their phones and didn't say a word to each other. Jemima pulled a trolley towards herself as soon as they walked into the supermarket.

"Doyin!" someone exclaimed and both girls turned to see a girl carrying a nylon walking towards them. She was obviously done shopping and Jemima wondered where she had seen the girl before.

"Heyy, What's up?" Doyin greeted back a bright look on her face that surprised Jemima.

"Oh, Jemima, meet Martha, Martha is Jemima" Doyin introduced and Martha smiled brightly at Jemima.

"Of course, I know you, I think more than half of CUA students do" Martha started and Jemima smiled lightly.

"Thank you" She didn't know if Martha was saying a compliment or was being sarcastic.

"You said you were coming to come and visit last month but you haven't even replied to my DM's not to talk of visiting" Marta accused Doyin who immediately grabbed her arm.

"I'm sorry huh" she whined hoping to make Martha forgive her.

"What about this, I'll follow you back home now?" Doyin suggested and Jemima furrowed her brows.

"I thought you came for shopping," Martha said and Doyin shook her head.

"I accompanied Jemima, she wanted to get some other things" Doyin replied as she turned to Jemima.

"Sorry I'm bailing on you, I really must go to Martha's place today. I'm sorry" she whined and Jemima nodded her head chuckling lightly

"It's okay. You can go with your friend" she replied and immediately started pushing her trolley cutting off whatever Martha had to say.

A frown marred Jemima's face as she filled up the trolley with cookies and chocolates. She couldn't exactly explain how she was feeling. Irritated? Annoyed? Betrayed? Lost? She couldn't exactly place her hand on it but she knew she wasn't feeling so good and Doyin and her recent antics were the cause.

She brought out her phone from her pocket and sent a message to the girls' group. There was a message from Ing saying that her article was featured in a Gossip Girl Magazine. She tapped on the link as she pushed the trolley around until she got to the Deoodrants session. A small smile graced her face as she scrolled through the article.

She had always known that Ing was gonna have her moment, something like this was going to help her resume so much.

"Jemima, is that you?"

Jemima turned to the voice and froze. She slowly dropped her hands to the sides as she stared at the duo in front of her. Black looked lazier than usual in his grey joggers and black T-shirt. He hadn't gotten a trim since the last time she saw him and a smile hung on his lips making him even more attractive but that exactly wasn't her problem, her problem was the person standing behind him.

She had promised herself not to have anything to do with him, she was going to run if she ever came across him but seeing the guy who looked absolutely irritated in front of her, his full lips pulled together in a flat line and her eyes lazy and bored, Jemima had no words to say.

A murderer shouldn't look this good. She shouldn't even be admiring a murderer in the first place. But hell, he looked damn good!

"Are you also...." she started returning her attention back to Black. Deep down she desperately wished that Black was just his driver. He wasn't part of the cult but she knew she was lying to herself.

"Are you also... Are you also..." Jemima was still unable to finish her sentence. Every single time she had met Black, every single scene played in her head and she would be an idiot if she couldn't connect the dots. Even an idiot could connect the dots. From the first day she had met him, she should have known.

"Do you want to ask him if I'm part of the Titans?" Black suddenly asked and Jemima froze. She didn't believe that he would have asked her so brazenly and so straightforward. She nodded her head slowly.

"Yes I am" he replied with a calm that made her stagger. She swallowed her saliva quietly releasing a breath she didn't know she was holding.

"You are a murderer too as well aren't you?" Jemima whispered but both men heard her loud and clear.

"Murderer?" Black asked with a frown and Jemima chuckled.

"You already admitted to being a part of them. Are you going to lie to me and say oh no, I haven't killed anyone ?" Jemima asked getting angry.

"When he was cutting those people's heads because they didn't want him to be the leader, what were you doing? Did you rat them out or did you give him the axe?' Jemima asked and the boy behind Black finally frowned.

"If I were you, I would clip my mouth because if you don't, you might end up facing the same fate as those people," he said in a smoky voice that sent tingles down Jemima's spine.

"I don't know where you heard that story Jemima but you really shouldn't believe everything you hear," Black said while Jemima opened her mouth to say something and suddenly remembered her conversation with Jeremiah. She closed her mouth and swallowed hard again, her gaze barely leaving the two men in front of her.

"I liked you. I trusted you" Jemima said quietly.

"Do you know how I felt when I found out who you were?" she asked and Black shrugged his shoulders.

"I have no idea but I'm quite used to this routine" he replied and Jemima knew that he meant people finding out that he was a cultist and not just a cultist, part of the Titans, the deadliest cult on campus.

"You don't think you owe me an apology?" Jemima asked raising her head to meet the two of them.

"Apology that I'm part of the Titans?" Black asked with a throaty chuckle.

"The least the both of you could have done was to tell me directly and I don't have to hear from other people," Jemima said and Black stared at her wide-eyed.

"They all knew, didn't they? Doyin knew, Paul and Peter, they knew who you were when you brought me that night but all of them including you decided to play me as the fool" She continued; chuckling and shaking her head.

"Will you really cut off my head; King?"

Someone should please hold Jemimah o, what do you mean by will he really cut off your head? But the woman is obviously angry and livid I mean there seems to be no other reason for that. I especially hate being kept in the dark and even more when everyone else knows what's going on, makes me feel stupid and foolish and that's exactly what everyone did to Jemima and she had every right to be livid.

There will be a poll, Question and Answer session on my IG story later this week, it should be on Thursday but anyway, watch out for it. It's gonna be fun and amazing.

Guess when the next chapter will be? If you guess right? It might just come at that time. Hehehe.

LOVE, your favorite writer.

23 | TWENTY-THREE |

THIS CHAPTER IS DEDICATED TO . YOU ARE AMAZING.

Jemima swallowed hard as soon as the question slipped from her lips. She didn't know Micah but had heard enough stories about him, and she knew for one that if he wanted her head off, he wouldn't hesitate to take it off. She shivered as soon as he started walking towards her, fear gripped her as she started walking backward.

"What are you doing?" she whispered.

"I'm Jeremiah's sister. He won't let you go if something happens to me" Jemima said again hoping to change Micah's mind.

She watched as he grabbed her trolley and turned to her, a blank look on his face "Do you want to get anything else?" he asked and Jemima froze, shock skimming through her face.

"I need toilet papers, new body sprays, and donuts" Jemima replied as as Micah turned to Black who nodded and then walked away. Jemima stared at the man in front of her in a daze.

"You aren't going to cut off my head?" she asked and Micah stared at her like she had grown a horn.

"Just shut up your mouth" Micah replied in a flat tone.

"You need to answer me. I need to talk to my parents and tell my friends goodbye" Jemima continued.

"I need to tell my roommates that I don't hate them and I know that they like me, I need to" Jemima continued rambling on, and suddenly Micah's face was directly in her face, merely inches away from hers. She drew in a breath as she watched his coffee-brown eyes bore lazily into her, his lips were pulled into an irritated line, his arched nose complimented his round face and she wanted to cup his face in between her palms badly.

"What part of shut up don't you understand?" he asked still watching her and Jemima folded her lips, humming words that sounded like I'm not going to say anything. Micah straightened up and rubbed his forehead.

"Pick your body spray," he said and Jemima nodded moving towards the shelf picking out her body spray putting it quietly in the trolley, and standing beside Micah. The latter glanced down at her before acting like he didn't see her.

"Why is he so tall?' Jemima murmured trying to stand on her toes.

"Jemima" Micah called in a way that made her swallow hard.

"Yes, yes, no talking" she replied immediately keeping quiet.

She watched as Black returned with everything she said she needed and placed it inside her trolley. Micah started pushing it towards the counter and Jemima followed behind, Black fell beside her and Jemima knew that he had something to say.

"I'm sorry Jemima" Black whispered and Jemima nodded her head.

"I know you do not like that apology. I'm sorry that I didn't tell you. I mean it" he added and Jemima sighed.

"Why didn't you tell me?" Jemima asked.

"And no don't say something like you thought I would run away" Jemima added and Black chuckled.

"Yes. That was part of it, I also really liked you yunno" Black replied and Jemima raised an eyebrow at him.

"Wouldn't you have run if I told you?' Black asked and Jemima found herself lost for words. Black was right, she would have done anything to avoid him.

"But the main reason was because it wasn't in my place to tell you. I hoped that Jerry would let you know" Black added and Jemima nodded her head.

She could see the stares and glances either people threw at them. There was a line but everyone rushed to the side upon seeing him and stepped to the side allowing Black to push both trolleys towards the cashier.

"Please pack up that trolley separately" Black instructed and the cashier nodded with a black face.

"Isn't that Jeremiah's sister?" she asked and Black nodded his head leaning against the wall while Jemima stared at the cashier surprised. Unlike other people, she seemed unbothered about Micah and Black.

"She knows?" she asked again and Black chuckled.

"En" Black replied and Jemima watched as the cashier threw a glance her way.

"That's surprising" she replied and Jemima scoffed.

"What's surprising?' she asked.

"That you are still here" she replied and Jemim rolled her eyes choosing not to reply. She threw a glance at Micah who was standing by the side and turned to Black.

"He's dying to have a smoke, isn't he?' she asked and Black burst into laughter.

"I have a good feeling about her" she whispered and Black turned to watch her face.

"About who? Jemima?" he asked and watched her nod her head.

"I swear, the feeling is so good and exciting" she replied and a small smile tugged at Black's lips.

"That's not a good thing," he said and the cashier merely laughed continuing to pack the goods they bought. Jemima watched as Micah stretched his card towards her and as she swiped it, handing him back a receipt and his card.

"Let's go," Black said and Jemima followed them out of the supermarket and Black turned to her again.

"Where are you going?" He asked.

"Back to the hostel" she replied.

"We are dropping her off?" Black turned to Micah to ask but it was more of a statement than a question and Jemima watched as Micah nodded his head without another word.

"C'mon get in" Black added after putting the nylons in the booth. Without another word, Jemima got into the backseat.

"You came alone?" Black asked and Jemima nodded her head. She wasn't about to tell Micah and Black how annoying or irritable Doyin had been acting these days. She watched as Micah produced a smaller pack of cigarettes from his pocket and a lighter already in his other hand.

"Can you wait till you drop before blowing some tobacco in my face?" she asked a bit airly frowning her face. Micah's movements were brought to a stop and he immediately dropped the cigarette in between his fingers without another word. She sighed pressing her back to the chair as silence descended on the car. Her eyes strayed to Micah and she realized that he was closing his eyes with a frown pulling apart his eyebrows.

"Can't you even smile in your sleep?" she whispered to herself before scoffing.

When the security guard saluted the car as they drove into school, she knew why they had done so this time around. Someone didn't have to tell her a lie or tell her she saw wrong. Jemima folded her arms underneath her breast and released a sigh she didn't realize she was holding.

Too much stimulating things had happened in recent days and she was yet to catch a break. Right from when she first met Micah, everything seemed to keep spiraling towards one end, an end she didn't know about. Jeremiah's words were still clawing at her mind and she was yet to make sense of it.

Why did Doyin, Paul, Peter, and Bimbo keep the fact that Black and King were members of the Titans? And that King was King- the leader of the Titans and Black - his right-hand man?

They had all met Black once even if they had never met King and they had all watched her make a fool of herself. Bimbo especially, Jemima had no doubts that Bimbo knew what was going on, why had she hidden it from her too?

"Does anybody have an idea why Heraline invited me to her party?" Jemima suddenly asked and Black glanced at her through the rear mirror.

"Heraline's party?" Black asked and Jemima nodded her head.

"You see there were too many coincidences. She didn't know either Doyin or me but she came to personally deliver our invitation cards, she gave it to Doyin but the person she wanted to get to was me" Jemima replied and Black glanced sideways at Micah whose eyes remained closed.

"And I found out later o, that I was probably the first nobody that almighty Hera had ever gone by herself to deliver an invitation card to" Jemima continued.

"It was just a party. She could have sent anyone, knowing it was her invitation, there was no way we would have missed it, either she sent it to me or Doyin but she came herself. Why? Because she needed 100% assurance that we were going to make it to the party" Jemima added chuckling.

"Don't you find that weird?" she asked and Black swallowed without replying.

"I hate mind games so much even though I'm freakish good at them. I hate being taken advantage of because of ignorance and put in the middle of some grand plan, either to speed it up or to serve as a cannon folder. I don't do such" the girl in the back seat continued and Micah's brows loosened.

The car rolled to a stop in front of her hostel and Jemima sighed softly.

"Are you going to tell me you don't know what I'm talking about?" Jemima asked suddenly.

"It does run in the family. You and your brother are smart. Clever" Black replied in a flat tone. Jeremiah had indeed told him that once Jemima discovered whoever they were, she was going to find out whatever Hera was planning.

Jemima watched as Black got out of the car after answering her, opening the booth, and bringing out her nylon. Jemima pushed the door open and collected the nylon from him. She rummaged through the nylon and brought out a pack of chocolates. She tore the pack open and brought out some pieces walking towards Micah's side of the car.

"This is for paying for my stuff," Jemima said and Micah finally opened his eyes and collected the pieces of chocolates. Their fingers barely touched but Jemima could feel the tinges that rushed down her feet when their hands grazed each other.

"You don't necessarily need to tell me what's going on, I will find out myself, I'm that smart" She finished turning on her heel and walking away.

"I also have zero idea what Heraline was thinking inviting her. I heard she and Jeremiah got into a huge fight" Black said and Micah withdrew his eyes from the girl who had already stepped into the hostel.

"Let's go check if Professor Farida is still on the school premises" Micah replied grabbing his abandoned cigarettes and lightening it. He slowly brought it to his mouth, took a drag, and blew wisps of smoke into the car.

"Whatever it is she's planning, I also want to see it"

Hello guys, so nice to see you guys again. This chapter was supposed to be up yesterday but I wasn't feeling so well and I'm much better now. And thank you StarHouse for the warm messages, I feel so much better. If You are not part of the StarHouse, you should know you are missing at this point.

What do you guys think about this chapter? Although I'm yet to reply to comments from the last chapter, I was really excited to read your comments and I'm super happy you guys were able to point out some of my thoughts, Jemima is moving worwor and some of y'all didn't even spare her face to call her out.

If you haven't realized after this chapter well I'll tell you, drama is about to start. I mean it's starting officially. From this chapter onwards, take note of everything you read because well, so you don't get confused or wonder when this happened or when that happened.

Thank you for your support guys. This little girl is grateful, super grateful.

Don't forget to click on that little star and commenttttt guysss, comment, it's gladdens my heart to see the commentsss.

24 'TWENTY-FOUR'

Black slowly drove to a stop in front of the Faculty of Medical Sciences. The cars in the car park were scanty, as the school day had long ended.

"Her vehicle is here; she is around," Black turned to face Micah, who gave a nod in agreement.

Black asked, "Are you going to take time?" Micah snorted in response.

As he put out his cigarette and got out of the car, he replied, "Time, my ass.". He grabbed one of the bars of chocolate Jemima had handed him and tore it open, biting into it as he walked into the faculty.

"Is Professor Farida in?" Micah asked the secretary, who nodded her head while staring at him in a daze.

"Do you have ..." Micah walked past her and opened the next door, shutting it behind him before she could finish.

The young lady in the office shot to her feet, raising her head and flashing a look of surprise across her eyes. She appeared to be younger than twenty-seven, with her slender figure adorned in a pair of perfectly fitting cream pantsuits. The light application of makeup further enhanced her appearance. The ends of her braids fell slightly above her shoulders, tightly coiled into ponytails.

She excitedly said, "You did not tell me you were coming," almost giving Micah a hug, but he slid past her arm motions without looking at her and sat down, crossing and stretching his legs on her table.

"Of course, how would you know? I blocked your number," Micah replied, immediately dousing the older woman's excitement. Farida swallowed quietly, sitting down in the seat next to Micah.

Nobody dared to treat her this way in her office; nobody dared to enter without an appointment; and nobody dared to enter so uninhibitedly that they had to put their legs on her desk. If anything, it made her want him even more because he was the only one who dared to do so. Even though he was six years younger.

"I'm sorry I spammed you with so many calls". She said softly, hoping to get an advantage, "I did not know you did not like it." She continued. She knew he wouldn't look for her or seek her out on a whim.

"You aren't sorry at all, are you?" Micah responded, and Farida felt her spine stiffen. Micah's voice had taken a flat tone. She had only heard it once in person and a lot of times in stories told by other people. He was angry.

"Bugging my boys and asking for my whereabouts, who gave you permission to do so?" Micah finally asked, his gaze meeting Farida's. The latter froze, opening her mouth repeatedly and failing to say anything.

"I.. I.. I.. I.. I.. I.. I." She kept repeating the same word over and over again. He would have her head in an instant, regardless of her feelings for him, provided she did not look for an excuse to follow his boys around and bother them. She couldn't have imagined that those boys would have told Micah or that he would be so protective of them. She had intentionally gone to look for Black at his faculty after her sources told her he was one of the fastest ways to get to him.

"I missed you!" she blurted out, proceeding to bat her eyelashes at him. She reached out and grabbed his free hand.

She said in a low voice, trying to gain sympathy, "I really missed you, but you would not even let me call you."

"Missed me?" Micah chuckled as he asked, and Farida nodded.

"I did miss you," she admitted.

"What part of me did you miss? My face? My dick? The sex? What exactly did you miss?" Micah inquired, and Farida stared at him, mouth agape. She didn't expect that Micah would be that straightforward.

"You aren't going to answer?" he asked again with a sneer at the edge of his lips.

"I missed everything about you. "The sex was also fantastic," she replied, choosing to be shameless until the end.

"You miss the sex," Micah said with a smile.

"I am sure you know, I do not sleep with the same woman twice," Micah stated flatly, and Farida swallowed her saliva while twirling her fingers around Micah's sleeve.

"There is always an exception to every rule," she replied coyly, and Micah burst out laughing, frightening Farida but she managed to hide her expression. She desired this boy so badly that it drove her insane, and she would do anything to have him. She did not care if he was the scariest and deadliest man in CUA; she wanted him and she was going to have him.

"You will not be that exception, even if there is one," Micah sneered, jerking his hands from her grip and biting into the open chocolates in his hand. He hissed slightly through his teeth; how did she like such sweet things? They were too sweet.

"I had no idea you liked chocolates," Farida said, and Micah slowly lowered his leg from the table, turning to face Farida squarely.

"Listen well and listen good," Micah began, and Farida felt her spine stiffen and straighten simultaneously.

"I will ruin you, and nothing, not even your grandfather, will be able to save you if I hear one more time that you are stalking any of my boys." Micah threatened, and Farida's eyes widened at the mention of her grandfather.

"How... How... How... Did you... Know?" she stuttered, and Micah smiled.

"If I know about your grandfather, that's enough proof for you to know that I can ruin you. "You better believe it," Micah replied, biting off the last of the chocolates and walking out of the office. He cleanly threw the wrapper of the chocolate into the dustbin as he walked out of the secretary's office.

"Gosh, she likes sweet things," Micah said to no one in particular as he climbed back into the car.

"Did she throw a tantrum?" Black asked with an amused smile as he reversed out of the parking lot.

"Tantrum? Can she?" Micah asked, chuckling as he lit another cigarette. Micah's mouth was left with a rather vague aftertaste from sucking on the tobacco and mixing it with the taste of chocolate he had just eaten. A small chuckle escaped his lips as he pressed down his chair and continued releasing a white wisp of smoke in the car.

"Greg sent a message, the Ravens are on the move," Black began, and Micah chuckled.

"Those guys do not know when to quit," Black added.

"He did not have specifics, but he believes they had something to do with Akande's problems." We received the lab results, and whoever raped that girl and Akande are two different people. Greg thinks the Raven has a hand in it. They threatened her with something we don't know yet and made her frame Akande. But it was entirely her choice to send her story to that ButterFly Fairy blogger," Black added, shaking his head.

"She's quite smart too. "Giving her story to an anonymous blogger on the school forum and then disappearing," he snorted.

"What part of, do not give me speculations, does Greg not understand?" Micah asked, closing his eyes.

"Tell the ones to raid the Ravens tonight. "Cart away everything, I do not want any deaths," Micah ordered, and Black grinned broadly.

"Yes, King," he snarled.

"With their recent aggressiveness, we have become too passive." They have raided two of our locations and we have remained silent; this time, they are in big trouble," Black said as he pressed the accelerator.

'What are we going to do about Akande's issue?" Black asked as he sped out of the school premises.

"Those guys like to act so self-righteous. It would be so nice for them to give us a blow or a handicap. Allow them to punish him however they see fit; do not interfere. Tell Akande to take whatever they give him quietly—an extra year or an extra semester or suspension—whatever those clowns come up with," Micah replied, and Black nodded his head.

"In the middle, we'll slam them with evidence, the lab reports. The school leaped to conclusions, so make sure it is big. It makes them less credible, and the board of directors should have a headache for quite some time. Then they will come to us for help," Micah continued, to which Black laughed and shook his head.

"Of course, we would be as unresponsive and unavailable as possible when they ask for our help," Black remarked, and Micah grinned.

"You know the drill. "Those damn fools always try to take advantage of any chance to mess with us," Black muttered as he pressed the horn, causing the gate to slide open. His phone rang almost immediately, and after seeing the caller ID, Black picked up the phone and put it on speaker.

"King," he said.

Micah's eyebrows furrowed into a frown as he answered, "Hmm."

"You are not going to like what I found."

Happy New Month lovessssss. Welcome to the month of November. I pray that we get plenty good news and plenty of updates. Amen.

Now that you guys have met Professor Farida, I want to hear your thoughts on her persona. Me, I already smell trouble and I hope you people are already smelling it. We had our Q & A on my IG story yesterday and some of y'all slyed me and didn't show up.

And as usual, I have dropped some many hints in this chapter, hopefully y'all pick it up. Thank you guys for 9k reads and 3k votes. I have a very funny goal for the month of November, let's get it!

Me I'm just curious as to who what that mysterious person found and told Micah he won't like. I can already smell drama.

And I felt so sweet when Micah kept complaining about how sweet the chocolates were yet he finished it. My heart practically melted. Ouuuu.

25 TWENTY - FIVE

Paul crossed his legs on the bed with his eyes closed, murmuring words that his roommates could not understand. He kept tapping his fingers on his belly in a rhythm. A few seconds after hearing his room door open, he felt the bedside gently press down on his legs. His eyes fluttered open slowly, and he saw a face that was a perfect reflection of his own.

"What is it?" he asked quietly, folding his arms and raising an eyebrow.

"I believe she now knows," Peter replied, a small smile on his face.

"That's interesting. How did she know?" He inquired, and Peter shook his head.

"I am not sure," he answered.

"How do you know that she now knows?" Peter shrugged in response to Paul's question.

"Well, she now knows. "What are we doing next?" he asked, and Paul sat up slowly on the bed, using the wall as a pillow and pulling his legs to himself.

"If she already knows, isn't she acting contrary to what we expect?" Paul inquired, and Peter rubbed his brow.

"I did tell you that it was risky to pin the success of the plan on her. "We do not know her," he responded, and Paul immediately frowned.

"Yes, and it was you who decided to go with the plan that pinned her with eighty percent success, remember?" Paul shot back at him.

"I told you that some information from her former classmates wouldn't be enough for us to ascertain what kind of person she is. "She is full of surprises; you can not even guess or imagine what she is thinking," he added, chuckling.

"She could even derail the plan," Paul said as he raised his head to meet Peter's.

He growled, "Shut up your mouth."

"You are not the only one who lost someone that day, Peter, so swallow whatever anger is creeping up your throat," Paul replied, and Peter let his back fall to the bed.

"So, what is next?" he inquired, and Paul sighed softly.

"If she knows, we should keep an eye on her movements for a while," Paul suggested.

"Should we try Bimbo?" Peter inquired abruptly, and Paul laughed.

"She knows enough that we could put her to use," he added.

"You think she's a joke? A girl with love all over her head?" Paul asked.

"For now, Jemima is our best bet. It might not work, but luckily we have a backup plan," he continued, and Peter nodded.

"What exactly do you think you are doing, Peter?" Paul inquired, and Peter turned to face him.

"What do you mean?" he asked, his brow furrowed.

"Vickie, Doyin," Paul replied with distaste in his mouth. His eyes were focused on the latter, scanning for any change of emotion. They were so familiar with one another that they could read each other's minds with a glance, and most of the time, Peter irritated him to the point where he occasionally found it impossible to breathe.

"You know we can not have her in the middle of this mess," Peter defended, and Paul burst out laughing.

"You and I both know what a terrible liar you are, Peter, so shove that excuse up your ass." Middle of this mess? I told you to let's cut her off even before we started this whole thing in the first place, but you refused. "She was already in the middle when we started this," Paul replied.

"And what dickhead move was asking Jemima to give Vickie your number?" he asked again.

"Jemima will tell either Jeremiah or Black what we told her, and they will know something is wrong because that is top-notch information, and whether we like it or not, she will start keeping things away from us." "Vickie is another way to find out what she is up to," Peter stated emphatically.

"So your new jerk move is to exploit someone else's emotions, right?" Paul and Peter immediately got irritated.

"Oh Paul, please, quit pretending to be Joseph. You understand better than anyone that we cannot achieve our goals by being two-goody shoes and being honest! If we were being honest in the first place, we wouldn't even be here!" he whispered-yelled.

"And you think you are going to be saintly in dealing with them? With him? He is the devil incarnate, and you have to be the devil to deal with a devil," he added, and a smile crawled up Paul's lips.

"There are a lot of people we could use Peter, I mean half of this school's students are not even innocent, but you want to use someone who knows nothing." She's innocent!" Peter scoffed as Paul whisper-yelled back.

"He was innocent too, wasn't he?" Peter asked, irritably looking at Paul.

"Paul, stop playing the saint card; you are not a saint." You don't even come close to it. "Not at all," he added, and Paul smiled without saying anything. He turned his head and looked out the window, a smile still on his lips.

"Do as you please, Peter. Do what you want."

"You can count on me to do whatever I want."

--

Jemima scrolled through the forum, a piece of chocolate in her other hand. She was not sure exactly what she was searching for, but for some reason, there was not a single news article about the Titians. There was a ton of news about the Ravens, the Claws, and other cults, but not even one post. Even just reading the news about the Ravens made Jemima's spine tingle because they were a rather large cult group.

If the Ravens were this dangerous and the Titians were twice as dangerous as they were, Jemima almost couldn't believe her eyes. She sent Adesewa a text immediately. Whatever Heraline or Black was trying to prove or achieve, she needed to find it fast. Being in the middle of something dangerous that she had no idea about was insane, but what was even more insane was the fact that she knew she was in something but could not even guess what it was.

The room door opened, and Vickie, Tamiloore, and Ayisat entered. She finally began to notice things she had not noticed before the day she overheard them. The cautious, inquisitive looks they gave her in two seconds, the double takes. A small chuckle escaped Jemima's lips as she stood up from her bed and walked towards Vickie.

"Give me your phone," she asked.

"Huh?" Vickie was clearly perplexed as to what was going on. Tamiloore and Ayisat exchanged puzzled glances.

"What do you want her phone for?" Jemima shrugged as Ayisat inquired.

"Would you give me your phone or not?" Jemima asked Vickie again, and she seemed to think for a few seconds before reaching into her pockets and pulling out her iPhone 14 Pro Max, which she handed to Jemima. Jemima took out her phone, and Vickie watched as she punched in a series of numbers and handed the phone over to her.

"Whose number is this?" Vickie inquired, puzzled.

"Peter's," Jemima replied, trying hard not to laugh.

"Pe... Pe... Pe what?" Vickie asked, her chest slamming into her ribs.

"Peter asked me to give you his number," Jemima replied, leaving Vickie speechless.

"Hey, do not fall off," she chided, and Vickie swallowed.

"Peter asked you to give me his number?' Vickie asked again. She was sure she wasn't hearing well.

"Yup. I told him you saw him carrying my bag and even picked a fight with me because you thought we were dating," Jemima replied, shaking her head.

She said, "I had to clear the air," as the latter gave her a horrified look.

"You heard us?' Tamiloore asked incredulously, and Jemima nodded.

"A little, but enough," she smiled in response.

"You could have directly asked me if we were dating or something," Jemima went on.

"Peter is handsome. There's no doubt about that. " He is charming, attractive, and adept at carrying on a conversation," Jemima said, to which Vickie sighed subtly.

"But he is not my type, not even close." We don't match or complement each other in any way. The same, I am sure, applies to him. Jemima finished.

Vickie blurted, "I am sorry," and Jemimah gave a quick nod.

"It's alright. "You guys are still dick heads," she replied as she walked into her bed and climbed into it, leaving the other three girls staring at the back of her head.

She wanted to jump up in excitement and laugh. She was aware that she had scared the three of them enough for the day. She wanted to console them but held back because of the nasty ways they treated her in order to hide the fact that they liked her.

Bunch of clowns.

She checked her chat window with Adesewa once more, but there was no message from her. Jemima tapped her tongue against her teeth and made a slight hissing sound. She hated being in the dark.

She detested it even more because this type of darkness was unfamiliar to her.

Hello everyone. I'm so sorry for the update delay. Due to some unforeseen circumstances, they couldn't go out as planned but here are they are anyways.

After this chapter, I know some people are finding coming for me. As for what Paul and Peter want? I don't know, you'll have to hang around to find out and Jemimah is such a funny person, see the way she scared them Vickie people.

And yeas, thank for the 10k reads on HOLDING YOU TIGHT. Lots of love from me to youuuu.

26 ' TWENTY - SIX '

J emima allowed her fingers to run through her thick hair as she listened to the young woman on the podium continue to explain something she could barely understand. Earlier that week, a survey form had been sent to the MBBS group, and they were asked to rate some of their lecturers and how much they enjoyed their classes and understood whatever they taught. In one day, about five of their lecturers had been swapped out, and one of their new lecturers was the famous Professor Farida Lawal.

A twenty-seven-year-old professor surely wasn't one you saw every day. She was well-known not only for becoming a professor at such a young age but also for her extremely attractive fashion sense and attractive face. She connected well with her students, and she had two classes with them since the change of lecturers, and Jemima herself admitted that she was a better lecturer than the previous ones.

Despite the fact that she took the time to explain a lot of things and sent them a lot of material, there were some things she did not understand. Jemima shook her head as her gaze swept over her dress. Today, she was clad in a navy blue fitted gown with kissing pleats at the edges. She styled the gown with a vintage scarf and wore boots to match. Her long wig fell on her shoulders, and her makeup was light but effective in capturing everyone's attention in class and keeping one's gaze fixed on her.

If not for her slightly mature face and the fact that she was a well-known professor, if she changed outfits and sat down in between them, they would think she was also a student.

"Does she look that good?" Paul inquired, and Jemima turned to face him, their faces inches apart, a smile on her face.

"Do not tell me you are not tripping hard for her?" Jemima inquired, and Paul shrugged his shoulders while maintaining eye contact.

"She does look good. "I do not like older women," he replied, and Jemima covered her mouth, laughing quietly.

"That is so mean, Paul," Jemima said quietly, and Paul shrugged once more.

"I need to see her after class," Jemima explained as she pulled out a piece of chocolate and bit into it. She extended it towards Paul, who turned his head immediately.

"I wonder how your gums and teeth are still intact. You do not even go to the gym, but you consume a lot of sugar. How is this chocolate your favorite?" Paul inquired, and Jemim muttered something he could not understand because she had chocolate in her mouth.

"You are a medical student, Jemi," Paul pointed out, and the response he got was Jemima throwing fake kisses at him. An amused smile tugged at his lips, and he shook his head, returning to his note-taking.

"You will receive the study materials, YouTube links, and PDFs in your email following this class; please read them carefully. "Please make sure you prepare adequately for your tests, which begin next week," Farida said in the hall, her voice clear and distinct.

"Failing my test is the fastest way to get on my bad side," she added, proceeding to close her laptop and slip it into her laptop bag.

"Then, good day, class," she finished with a smile, turning and exiting the classroom.

Jemima flung her books into her bag and hurried after Farida. She had a few questions for her. She could hear Paul rushing after her.

"Professor Farida!" Paul yelled for Jemima, who was still eating the chocolate.

Farida turned, and the first thing she saw was a much younger girl with flawless and perfect skin, bright eyes, and a crop top that barely showed off her stomach because she was wearing a high waist skirt, but it exposed the waist beads that graced her perfect waist. Farida could swear that she had almost never seen a more perfect body. But something else had piqued her interest: the chocolate in her mouth, which was so familiar that it only took her a second to recall where she had seen it.

Paul approached the duo and immediately pulled the chocolate into Jemima's mouth, causing Jemima to cough lightly.

"Good afternoon Professor Farida, my name is Jemima Adeleke, an MBBS student, and I have a few questions about what you just taught us," Jemima said calmly, staring at Farida.

"Where did you get those chocolates?" Farida inquired, her gaze shifting from Paul to Jemima. Jemima stared at her in surprise.

"At the supermarket outside school," Jemima replied, exchanging puzzled looks with Paul.

'When?" Farida asked, and Jemima furrowed her brows.

"I can not remember exactly, but it was last week," Jemima replied.

"Is there a problem, Professor Farida?" Jemima asked carefully, and the latter sneered, much to Jemima's surprise.

"Your name and matriculation number?" Farida inquired.

"Jemima Adelek, MBBS/22/3102" Jemima replied and watched as Farida nodded her head.

"As for your questions, I already told you; you will get study materials in the mail," she said to the pair before walking away, leaving Jemima and Paul staring at each other.

"Do you have any idea what just happened?" Jemima asked, and Paul shrugged.

"I swear I heard her sneer at you," Paul said, and Jemima nodded.

"Nahh, you were not the only one who heard that," she added, taking back her chocolates and biting into them. She turned to face the direction Farida had walked away from and watched as she got into her car and drove out of the parking lot.

"She asked for my matriculation number, which is not a good sign. I'm in trouble for eating a bar of chocolate while trying to talk to her." Jemima asked as Paul relieved her of the tote bag.

"That's not much of a big deal. She is not that evil. Paul immediately dismissed Jemima's concerns, and the latter nodded.

"She sounded so irritated as she said, "Like I said before, there will be study materials in your mail; please consult them," Jemima mimicked, and Paul burst out laughing.

'We have practicals, let us get going,' Paul said, and Jemima nodded, biting the last bite of her chocolate and dumping the nylon.

Jemima couldn't wait to get back to the hostel; she fell onto her bed and slept off almost immediately. She was tired and hungry; aside from the chocolates she had managed to cram into her stomach before the practical, she had not eaten anything all day. Doyin had gone to see another of her friends off campus, so there was no one to feed her.

By the time she woke up, it was a few minutes past 11 p.m.; her stomach grumbled, and everyone in the room turned to her. They had somehow gotten to a level of tolerance and calm in the room, so Jemima immediately waved her hands to apologize.

"Sorry guys," she apologized, holding her stomach. She was starving and knew that eating custard or cereal would not satisfy her stomach. She needed to eat real food, but it was past 11 p.m., the hostel doors closed at midnight, and the schools' eateries were nearly a twenty-minute walk from the hostel, a total of forty minutes to and fro, even if she got her order as soon as she got to wherever she wanted to order, which was nearly impossible.

"Well, I got you food earlier," Vickie interrupted Jemima's thoughts by extending a packaged box to her.

"You got food for me?" Jemima asked, surprised, as she took the box from Vickie, who nodded.

"There is this guy in your department who likes to talk to me," Vickie replied, her voice tinged with pride.

"He messaged me when you guys finished your practical. I saw you walk into the room and sleep off, so when I went out to get food earlier, I just got one extra in case you woke up late," Vickie explained, and Jemimah smiled.

"Thank you very much," she thanked Vickie sincerely opened the box to find a packaged plate of fried rice, peppered turkey, and salad.

"Goshh Vickie, you know what I would like," Jemima cooed, tearing into the peppered turkey first. Her eyes narrowed in surprise.

"Where did you get the turkey?" Everyone in the room laughed when Jemima asked amidst mouthfuls.

"It is bad table manners to stuff yourself and talk at the same time, Jemimah." Vickie chastised her before getting out of bed and taking a bottle of water from her wardrobe, unscrewing it, and placing it beside Jemimah's legs.

"You are a darling," Jemimah said, taking two gulps from the bottle.

"But where did you get it? "It is better than most of the peppered turkey I buy," she asked once more.

"Social Mavins," Vickie replied, drawing a raised eyebrow from Jemima.

"Social Mavins?" she asked.

"We only buy food from them. "They make the best savory food," Tamiloore replied, and Jemima nodded.

"I should give them a try then."

"The good news is that you have already done so."

I can't believe I'm loving the dynamics between Jemimah and her room-mates. Who would have thought? I want to insert like two hundred memes and emojis to express myself right now but well since I can't, hehehehe.

Trouble is brewing o. Hehehehe.

27 TWENTY - SEVEN

One week later, both Paul and Jemima realized they were mistaken. They were wrong about Jemima not being in trouble. Professor Farida taught them two different courses, both of which made Jemima's life a living hell. Everyone had one question on their minds: In what way had Jemimah offended Professor Farida?

Even within the department, she was quiet and reserved; she was never the center of attention. She seldom spoke in the group. Someone like that could never have irritated Professor Farida; their senior counterparts had told them that Professor Farida was very cool and that it was difficult to get on her bad side, and they had confirmed that in two classes, but after that it was an onslaught of attacks on Jemima for no apparent reason.

Jemima pursed her lips as Professor Farida walked out of the class in long, elegant strides. She knew better than to follow her. Every single one of her attempts to do so previously had proven futile. The latter wouldn't see her, so there was no way she could even find out why the other woman was being so bitchy to her.

"Are you okay?" Paul asked with a small frown on his face. Jemima turned to him with a blank face.

"Do I look okay to you?" she asked, folding her arms and ignoring the curious and questioning looks from the other students. She would be surprised if they did not look at her that way; if she were someone else, she would definitely look at herself that way.

"I just want to know what I did to her other than talk to her with a piece of chocolate in my mouth," Jemima muttered quietly, rubbing her brows.

To say Professor Farida's onslaught of questions and attacks on her didn't affect her would be an understatement. She initially thought the latter was genuinely asking her questions, but it did not take long for her to realize that the latter was deliberately targeting her, which made no sense to her. She had done nothing at all.

"Are you sure you have never met her in town or something before?" Paul asked as they walked to the hostel.

"You have asked that a thousand times and Paul, I still have the same answer for you, I haven't," Jemima said, rolling her eyes. "I had no idea who she was until she started teaching us, okay?"

"Let us hope she gets over her bias and marks your test script correctly." Paul said, and Jemima rolled her eyes once more. "She better do," she said.

And yet again, Jemima and Paul were proven wrong. Jemima gazed at her test script, which had a big zero and a line comment written on top.

You need to read the questions properly before answering them.

A small chuckle escaped her lips as she walked out of the lecture theater with everyone staring at the back of her head.

"Jemimah!" Paul yelled after her, but she was unconcerned. Jemima's heart burned fiercely in her chest. She did not care if Professor Farida bitched at her and singled her out in class; she had put up with enough of her ridiculous behavior. When she was only in her first year, she was even forced to answer postgraduate questions. But her tests? That was a no-go area.

Even if Jemima wrote an impromptu test, there was no way she would get a zero, but she had given her a zero on a test she had over-prepared for. Jemima was sure that Professor Farida hadn't even read her answers at all.

How could someone be so spiteful and bitchy at the same time?

Jemima pushed open her office door and entered. "I want to see Professor Farida," she said to the secretary, who looked at her in surprise. The girl in front of her looked familiar, but she was different; her eyes were red, and anger was written boldly on her face.

"Professor Farida is busy, please return later," the secretary responded, looking through her files and pulling out the visitor slip before placing it in front of Jemima. "You can fill out the form and I will pass it across to her," the secretary added, and Jemima burst out laughing.

"How many of those visitor slips have I filled?" she asked. "Should I remind you?" she asked again.

"Are you stupid, or are you pretending to be stupid?" Jemima barked at the secretary, and a frown crept up her face in an instant.

"Excuse me, young lady, please mind your words," the secretary replied. Jemima had yet to respond when the door opened and Professor Farida stepped out of the office.

"What's going on here?" She raised her nose to ask, and Jemima was so annoyed that she nearly burst out laughing.

"Oh, it is you," she continued, smiling.

'Professor Farida, you didn't even read my answers. I should read the questions properly before answering." Jemima inquired, a wry grin spreading across her face.

"Should I go back to the class and bring everyone's script and compare our answers together and confirm if I read the questions before answering?" Jemima inquired once more, and Farida grinned.

She said in a monotone, "You are going to carry over this course," and turned to leave.

Jemima's phone buzzed in her pockets, so she took it out. When she saw the caller ID, she swiped the accept call button and held the phone to her ears.

"Hey sweetie," Jeremiah cooed over the phone, but the next second he heard whimpers from the other girl.

"Jemimah?" Jeremiah called nervously, and the whimpers grew louder.

"Jemima, are you crying?" He inquired, and Jemima tried unsuccessfully to wipe the tears from her cheeks. She ducked under one of the trees, hugging her knees and sobbing.

"Jemima, where are you?" Jeremiah inquired once more, his voice worried.

Jemimah had rarely cried since they were children. He was the crybaby of the house, not Jemimah. For whatever reason she was crying, Jeremiah didn't dare to imagine it.

"She.... said..... I would... carry over the course," Jemima replied between whimpers, a frown spreading across Jeremiah's face.

'Who said so? "What happened?" he inquired, but Jemimah continued to whimper. He sighed slowly and allowed the latter to calm down before speaking. By the time Jemima was done explaining, Jeremiah had a strange look on his face.

"Is there a way I can report her? "I would like to report her," Jemimah said, and Jeremiah swallowed.

"Let me get back to you. "Give me a few minutes," Jeremiah said, and Jemimah whimpered quickly before hanging up. She threw her head backward while wiping her tears. She hadn't realized how much what had happened had taken a toll on her until Jeremiah had called.

"Fuck you, Farida."

———---

Jeremiah hung up the phone and turned to face the man who had already locked his gaze on him, his eyes demanding an explanation.

"What happened to Jemimah?" Jeremiah swallowed as Black asked, concerned.

"You won't say anything?" Jeremiah cleared his throat as King asked.

Jeremiah winced and said, "She has some ties to you."

Connected to King? Black asked in surprise.

"Who has ties to King?" he asked again.

"Professor Farida "Jeremiah answered, and Black started giggling.

"Ties my ass. What has Professor Farida got to do with Jemimah?" When Black questioned once more, Jeremiah parted his lips to answer.By the time he was done repeating what Jemimah had told him, Black had a murderous look on his face.

"Jemimah wants to report her. I know she will not be able to submit it, but is there any way you could assist her in speaking with Professor Farida?" Jeremiah asked while fixing a serious gaze on King.

"Wait, she was eating chocolates when she first met Professor Farida?" Jeremiah nodded as Black inquired.

"That is what she said," Jeremiah replied, and Black turned to face King.

"What are the coincidences? He chuckled, "King, this time around, you are responsible," he added, and Jeremiah furrowed his brow.

"Responsible for what?" he asked.

"Tell Jemima not to worry, we will figure it out," Black said as he rubbed Jeremiah's back.

"Go meet Jemimah; she is probably on her way to the hostel." "Get her some food and those chocolates she really likes," he said, and Jeremiah nodded.

"Thank you, King," he said with a relieved smile. He had heard from others that something was going on between King and Professor Farida, so when Jemimag told him what had happened, he was hesitant to tell King to help.

Black turned to King with a smile as Jeremiah walked out of the room. "She is really asking for death, is not she?" he asked.

"What should I do?" Black inquired as King drew a long drag on his cigarette. He puffed out a large amount of smoke, masking his face and expression; Black could feel the hair on his body standing the next second.

"I will take care of it myself."

Hello my people; HAPPY NEW MONTH! It's so glad to be back here although some of you guys will be rolling your eyes a bit. I did tell StarHouse that updates would be dropping on the first of this month and somehow today is fifth. My apologies.

I feel so sorry for Jemima and what she is going through. Professor Farida is just looking for trouble at this point and unluckily for her, she has successfully kicked the hornet's nest so whatever happens to her, serves her right.

I can't believe Jemimah cry, hard girl don dey cry.

DON'T FORGET TO VOTE AND COMMENT! GUYS, PLEASE COMMENTTTT!

THANK YOU.

28 TWENTY - EIGHT

More wisps of smoke covered the atmosphere, hiding his expression and face, and Black could feel his hair standing on its ends. His eyes widened in surprise once more. King was enraged; livid would be a better word.

He was aware of Jeremiah's significance to him, which implied that Jemimah was also significant to him. Although she was unaware of it, someone was constantly watching over the latter from the shadows, safeguarding her from the moment she set foot in CUA, per King's order. This time, she had been implicated because of him, and she had broken down in such a way that worried him, and now they had discovered that King was the cause.

"Are you angry at yourself for not being careful?" Black inquired, leaning back in his chair and stretching his leg. He had no doubts that King would swing his leg at him the next moment for asking such a question. King despised mistakes, and now he had made one that had landed Jemimah, someone innocent in hot water.

"Are you looking for trouble?" Micah asked back, and Black felt his spine straighten.

"What are you going to do?" he asked again.

"Ask the boys to check if she is still in her office," Micah said monotonously, dropping his cigarette in the ashtray next to him.

"Okay," Black said, pausing and weighing whether to continue speaking, "it is not your fault, at least not entirely your fault, that Jemimah is trouble. Who would have guessed that freak of a Professor would notice some damned chocolates? And what were the coincidences that Professor Farida would start taking some of her classes and the coincidence that she was eating that same chocolate while speaking to her?" Black asked no one in particular, shaking his head.

"Gosh, this woman is nuts. What if Jemima had also bought the chocolates out of the blues and didn't even know you?" He kept asking, which seemed to worsen Micah's mood.

"Abraham," Micah said, and Black bolted from his seat and out the door.

Micah stared wordlessly at the bolting figure and threw his head backward. As his coffee-brown eyes remained fixed on the ceiling, no one could guess what was going through his mind. A hiss escaped his lips, and then a familiar face peered through the door.

"King, she is at the office," Black's voice said, and Micah leapt to his feet.

"Start the car," he said as he walked down the hall toward his room. He opened the wardrobe and grabbed one of the shirts, pulling his arms through it without butting at all.

By the time he stepped outside, Black had driven the car towards the gate. Someone shut the door behind him after he opened it. Black didn't think twice before pressing down on the accelerator and speeding out of the compound. He cast a sidelong glance at Micah, who was staring at him blankly. His previous murderous aura had vanished, but Black knew better. This boss of his had something planned in his head.

"What are you going to do when we get there?" Black inquired, and Micah maintained his blank expression.

"What do you think I should do?" Micah inquired, and Black groaned inwardly. Micah replying to his questions with questions was something King did whenever he had something dangerous planned in mind. He shuddered quietly while shaking his head.

"It is up to you, King," he said, his side glance catching the tips of Micah's lips tilting and almost slamming on the brake. He drove slowly into the Faculty of Medical Sciences and parked the car. Micah got out of the car and took long strides towards Farida's office, his shirt flapping in the wind behind him. Black knew Micah was going to take Professor Farida's head off, so he jogged to catch up.

She had dared to do something that no one else had. She had punished someone for eating the same chocolates as King, and unfortunately for her, the girl was King's school's younger sister. She had not only picked on her in class, but she had also failed her. Black shook his head repeatedly at her foolishness.

When the door was flung open, the secretary raised her head in annoyance and opened her mouth to speak sense to the latter, but the words became stuck in her throat when she met Micah's cold eyes. Words formed in her mind, but even with her mouth open, she could not say anything.

She could feel the murderous atmosphere the moment Micah walked in, and she had only one thought. How had her boss offended this god of death?

Micah was unconcerned about the secretary, who was frozen in her seat with her mouth wide open; he pushed open the second door without hesitation. Farida raised her head in annoyance at the person who had not knocked and pushed the door open, her eyes widening in surprise, a sweet smile spreading across her lips, and her eyes curving in crescents.

She knew it; she knew he would return. She knew her abilities the best after all.

"King! It is a pleasant sur..." Micah closed the gap between them and clasped his thin yet firm and long fingers around Farida's neck, pinning her against the wall before she could finish her words.

Farida's eyes widened in shock. She knew something was wrong when her hands clutched Micah's hands as she gasped for air, and one look at Miach told her he was angry. She was in soup!

"How dare you?!" Micah asked, enunciating each other in a way that made all of Farida's bones feel cold.

"How dare you touch her?" Micah inquired once more, chuckling.

"Who do you think you are? Who do you think you are to treat her like that?" Micah continued firing questions as his fingers continued to tighten around Farida's throat. The latter had a lot to say, she wanted to beg but more than anything she wanted to live, she could feel the air being sucked out of her throat, her head was getting dizzy, and as a doctor herself, she knew it was because of a lack of oxygen to her head.

Her gaze shifted to the other boy in the room, who was leaning against the wall; a glance at him and she knew he would not help her.

"Carryover? "You do talk big," Micah observed, as Farida coughed and pulled on Micah's arm, but his arm did not even bulge.

"Ki...Ki....King.. ple....plea....please" In an instant, Micah released his grip on Farida's throat, causing her to collapse to the ground while struggling to breathe. She repeatedly patted her chest, as though she was breathing in more oxygen than she needed. Micah leaned forward and gazed at her slowly.

"You wanted to give her a carry-over since we both ate the same chocolates," Micah questioned, and Farida leaned against the wall, her hands shaking and her clothes drenched from perspiration. She had fear in her eyes. She should have known, she should have known, that his reputation as the devil did not come simply because he said it. She thought she was going to pass out from being choked for a moment.

She should have avoided him, but the unwillingness in her heart had not gone away; her eyes were fixed on him like a hawk, obsession in her eyes. She desired this man at all costs, even if it meant risking her life. She would do anything to get his attention, to have him take another look at her.

"What does she have that I don't? "I even have a better figure than she does," Farida said, her chest slowly heaving up and down.

"Was she better in bed than I was?" Farida inquired, but her words were barely out when Micah's left hand swung at her.

Pah!

The sound was so loud in the room that Black swallowed. This woman really didn't know what was good for her. Even daring to malign Jemimah when she had almost lost her life seconds before.

Farida could feel her cheeks burning and her eyes widening as she stared at Micah. He had slapped her, and he had done so without hesitation. No one had dared to touch her in her entire twenty-seven years of existence; she was her father and grandfather's cherished daughter, but Micah had gone ahead and delivered a slap that she could still feel the stinging sensation after minutes.

"You don't know what's good for you?" Micah inquired, his coffee-brown eyes darkening with rage.

"You slapped me for her?" Farida inquired, and Black sighed. She was done for.

"I guess she was that good in bed," she added, watching as Micah dropped his head and the chill in the room seemed to rise a few notches. Farida felt her spine straighten in fear. She had misspoken!

Micah slowly raised his head, and the anger in his eyes had faded, replaced by his usual blank expression, which terrified Farida. She watched as he slowly straightened up and looked down at her like he was looking at an ant.

"Professor Farida, I think the Dean would agree with me if I suggested that you take a sabbatical and get a job at your father's university in Amsterdam," Micah said clearly, and Farida's eyes widened in horror.

"King!" she exclaimed in shock.

"By tomorrow morning, you should be on a flight to Amsterdam or at the airport. By now, it will be difficult to obtain an early morning ticket," Micah continued, turning to leave, but Farida grabbed his leg.

"King, please, I promise you. "Please do not send me away. I will not go near her and I will not come near you. I would stand still and stay still and make myself invincible." The older woman had tears running down her cheeks. Her body was trembling, and the perspiration had caused her suit to stick to her body.

"You threw it in my face when I gave you a chance," Micah laughed in response.

"You should have had second thoughts when she came here repeatedly begging you and crying, but you did not care," Micah said as he walked out of the room and stopped at the door without looking back.

"And lest I forget Abubakar Farida, I dare you, I dare you, I dare you to call your grandfather."

Double update! Yes!

I have no words for Professor Farida at this point, what kind of obsession is this? Ha. She had it coming but I feel so sweet insideeee. If my man would do this for me, make he stay away from me o. ehn ehen

Some people's opinion of King would have taken a 360 turn after this chapter but i know you still love him!

DON'T FORGET TO VOTE AND COMMENT!

29 TWENTY - NINE

B lack looked at King strangely as he extended his hand towards him. "Do I need to repeat myself?" he asked, raising an eyebrow and dropping the car key into his palms.

"You are going to apologize?" Black inquired, but King refused to respond and got into the car.

Black slipped his hands into his pockets and watched as Micah reversed and drove out of the compound. "It is not like I will laugh at him when he is apologizing," Black said, chuckling. "That would be a sight to see, though," he added before pulling out his phone and dialing a number.

"Come and pick me up at school; your boss has graciously left me to fend for myself," Black grumbled, and a female voice entered his ears.

"Then fend for yourself," and the call was abruptly terminated. Black stared at the phone after hearing the beep sound and burst into laughter.

"I need to report all of them, they are taking me too lightly," he said to no one in particular before turning his gaze to the building behind him.

"Hopefully she grows a brain in Amsterdam," Black added as he walked away, his hands in his pockets.

Micah telling her to leave him was completely unexpected. He knew the latter was going to do something extreme, like publicly apologize to Jemima, but Farida had consistently ruined her chances; if she had apologized and remained silent the first time, maybe she would have gotten off, but she took her chance to live and, as Micah put it, she flung it in his face that she did not need it.

"Anyways, if he left her alone, she would find another way to stir up trouble for Jemimah. It is a good thing she is leaving," he said as a car stopped in front of him. The glass was lowered, and a very attractive young lady sat in the driver's seat.

"You came!" Black exclaimed joyfully as he opened the door and got into the car.

Jemimah froze the moment his voice entered her ears and sat up on her bed, ignoring the tremor that ran through her body when she heard his voice.

"You are?" she asked again to be sure.

"King," the other replied simply.

"I am outside your hostel," he added before hanging up.

Jemima stared at her phone, blinking rapidly. King was looking for her. For what? She walked out of bed, pulling a roundneck over her head. Various thoughts raced through her mind, but she came to one conclusion: Jeremiah has informed King of her predicament. When she stepped out of her hostel, there was no King in sight, but seeing the black Camry parked by the side, even though her glasses were tinted, she knew it was him.

She got into the car by opening the door to the front passenger seat and closing it behind her. Maybe because she had cried her eyes out earlier,

Jemimah wasn't thinking of running away from him. She was tired and moody.

"Hello," she said, trying to smile. A small frown crawled up Micah's face after she greeted him.

"Are you okay?" he inquired, and Jemima allowed the air conditioning in the car to blow against her. She reached for the lever beside the chair and yanked it back, allowing the carseat to recline.

"Sort of," Jemima replied. She was more than sure that Jeremiah had informed him.

"I'm sorry about what happened. "I will take care of it," Micah said, and Jemima turned to face him, one of her eyebrows raised.

"I am half to blame for your predicament," Micah added, but Jemima did not bother asking what he meant. If he said he was going to take care of it, Jemima had no doubts that he was going to. The cold air blowing against her made her sleepy, and because she had cried earlier, the sleepiness weighed heavily on her.

"Thank you," she muttered quietly, closing her eyes briefly.

Micah watched as the girl closed her eyes, her lashes fluttering quietly. Even though she had cleaned her face, he could still see the tears welling up in her eyes. Her face was etched with stress lines, and he rubbed his glabella slowly, annoyed.

"Hey," he said to the girl next to him, but he got no response. Micah chuckled as he looked at her again; she had fallen asleep. He pushed his chair back and took out his phone, intently scrolling through his lengthy document.

Jemima had no idea how much time had passed, but when she opened her eyes, the first thing she saw was Micah scribbling on a piece of paper with a small frown on his face. Upon glancing at his notes, she instantly recognized that they contained engineering mathematics. Aside from being the deadliest cultist, he was still a student.

"Awake?" This time, Jemimah was unable to ignore the tremor that ran through her when Micah's voice drifted back into her ears. Her ears seemed to itch for some reason.

"How long did I sleep?" Jemimah asked. By her calculations, she didn't sleep for a long time.

"A little over an hour," Micah answered, keeping his head buried in the paper he was scrawling on.

"Is that an assignment?" Jemimah asked quietly.

"No," Micah replied, and Jemimah watched as he finally turned to face her. She took a glance at what he had written and realized that she couldn't understand a single thing.

"You look after yourself, Choco," Micah said, widening Jemimah's eyes in surprise.

"Choco?" she asked and Micah nodded his head.

'You love chocolates, don't you?" he asked and Jemimah snickered.

She sighed and said, "And it somehow landed me in trouble okay," to which Micah nodded.

He inquired once more, "So you have stopped eating chocolates since then right?" to Jemimah's amusement.

"No way," she said, meeting Micah's coffee-colored eyes with a startled laugh.

"Okay, okay. "That is a strange nickname, though," she continued.

"You'll get used to it," Micah defended and Jemimah nodded her head.

"Thank you for coming to see me." She was touched by the gesture.

"You look after yourself," Micah said. Jemimah nodded and stepped out of the car, slowly walking into the hostel.

Her head felt light but her thoughts were already starting to take shape. Even if Jeremiah had reported the issue to King, she didn't think it was enough for him to come to her hostel to come and see her. She turned just in time to see King drive away and she chuckled softly before resuming her walk back into the hostel.

Something told her whatever might have happened to her might have something to do with King but she had no evidence. Even though King's apology hinted that he was involved, it was not enough for her to assume. And even if it had something to do with King, what exactly did it have to do with him?

Jemima quietly pushed the room door open and opened her wardrobe; she could not believe she had fallen asleep in King's car while the latter had just gone ahead to begin working on engineering Mathematics. She had no idea he was that patient; the rumors she had heard about him told her he wasn't.

Was she enjoying all of this because she was the younger sister of his school son? Didn't that make her his school daughter?

Jemimah immediately frowned at her last thought. She certainly didn't want to be his school daughter.

"School daughter, my feet," Jemimah said to herself, her frown deepening as the words left a terrible aftertaste on her lips.

Even though she was hungry, none of the cereals and snacks in her wardrobe seemed to be calling to her. Her phone buzzed again in her pockets, she took it out, and her eyes widened in surprise.

I forgot to inform you but I ordered food for you while you were sleeping. The driver just called, and he should be in front of your hostel.

Jemimah had just finished reading the text when she received a call from an unknown number; she swiped the green call and pressed the phone to her ears.

"Hello, I am outside with an order for you."

——---

The next day left Jemimah further in shock and surprise. The moment she stepped into the lecture theatre, she noticed that almost everyone was looking at her weirdly. Paul turned to her with a small frown.

"Why do I feel everyone is looking at you weirdly?" he asked and Jemimah nodded her head.

"You do not feel, everyone is actually looking at me strangely," Jemima responded, and they had not even sat down when the Class President appeared in front of her.

"Good morning, Jemimah," he said, uncertainly looking at her.

"Good morning," Jemimah replied, wondering what the Class President wanted with her.

"Could you please hand over your PHARM 101 script?" "I have to hand it over to the new lecturer for marking," said the Class President, and Jemimah looked at him as if he had two heads.

"New lecturer? Who is this new lecturer? Startled, she questioned. The class president furrowed his brows as he saw Jemimah's expression of surprise and shock.

"You really didn't know they changed lecturers? "I thought you reported Professor Farida." The class President responded directly, silencing the entire hall.

"Report? "I have yet to do that," Jemimah responded. Her response elicited small whispers and discussions in the hall.

"She hasn't reported?'

"So someone else reported Professor Farida?"

"That's crazy"

"How hasn't she even reported? Professor Farida was being very unjust to her."

"Someone said it because Professor Farida could not stand the fact that she was so attractive."

"That is okay; it is childish."

"Explain to me what happened," Jemimah said, ignoring the conversations and comments going on around her.

"Well, late yesterday I received an email informing me that we had a new lecturer and that I needed to report to his office today with your script to be remarked. I believe they also sent you an email." Jemimah stared at the class President as he responded, trying to take in what he had said.

"I have not checked my mailbox yet," she admitted.

"Wait, what about Professor Farida?" Jemimah inquired, and the Class President laughed.

"Honestly, I find it difficult to believe that you have nothing to do with this Jemimah, but seeing you now, I guess I was wrong," he said, folding his arms.

"I heard she took a sabbatical and that she will not be returning." There's a chance that she's going to take up lecturing at a private university in Amsterdam," he added and Jemimah opened her mouth like a fish brought out of water.

"Oh, please, can anyone just take a sabbatical like that?" She inquired, and the class president shrugged.

"I guess they all don't dislike you like they pretend to do. Someone reported you to the school authorities on your behalf, and whoever it was had to have some sort of connection. "Your luck jar is quite full," he replied, and Jemimah laughed.

"I did not bring my script today; can I bring it tomorrow?" She asked and the class president nodded.

"Sure, I will notify the lecturer,' he said as he walked away.

"What are the chances?" Paul murmured, staring at Jemima's dazed expression. The girl was clearly shocked and surprised; no one would doubt that she knew something about it.

Jemimah sat down slowly and chuckled; King; was this his handiwork?

Jemimah held the nylon in her hands tighter. There was no way she could have explained what she was doing if someone had asked her. When she first learned about King, she was so terrified that she made a self-promise to never go near him. She had promised herself to stay clear of him and the Titans.

She had been afraid that her brother was a member of the Titians and believed that he was also a murderer when she learned that he had connections to them. And after he cleared up the air, she even further resolved to stay clear of them but somehow, their paths kept crossing.

And now, she was standing in front of her hostel waiting for him and holding a bag of chocolates as thank you for him. When she had sent him a text message earlier asking him if he had time to come and see her at her hostel, she hadn't thought he would reply at all and even if he did, he would refuse but surprisingly, he had replied and asked her when it would be comfortable for him to come and see her.

A familiar car rolled to a stop in front of Jemimah and she opened the door and got in. Jemimah turned to greet the other boy and immediately sucked in her breadth. She had seen him so many times but each other, she was left dazed by his appearance. How could someone be so..... Ridiculously handsome, sexy effortlessly without doing anything.

Micah was clad in hue colored shirt with his hands folded to his elbow, and the crisp white roundneck he wore underneath hid his upper body. His coffee-brown eyes quickly met her gaze and Jemimah coughed awkwardly trying to hide her embarrassment.

"This is my thank you," Jemimah said handing over the nylon in her hands to Micah. The latter collected the nylon and opened it. He threw his head backward and turned to Jemimah with an amused smile.

"You don't like chocolates?" Jemimah asked. Micah watched the girl in front of him ask him a question, an amused smile still on his lips. He glanced at the same chocolates that caused her trouble and shook his head.

"I don't mind" his deep voice immediately dispelled her thoughts and Jemimah heaved a sigh of relief.

"Thank you for what you did. I'm not going to ask you how you did it and what happened" Jemimah started and King nodded his head.

"That's very smart" Micah replied in a calm way that made Jemimah shiver.

"Did you have classes today?" She asked trying to make small talk. Micah was always calm and quiet around her, It was hard to decipher what he was thinking.

"Yes, but I only attended one of them" Micah replied bringing out the chocolates and unwrapping it. He bit into it and shook his head lightly. He really couldn't understand her love for sweet things, the chocolates were too sweet.

"You are too busy to attend classes?" Jemima probed again and Micah nodded his head.

"Something like that" Micah replied and Jemimah furrowed her brows.

"Aren't you worried it's gonna affect your grades?" she inquired again and Micah turned to face her again; his eyes taking in her concerned face.

"You don't need to worry about my grades" A small smile spread to his lips.

"Oh. I see" Jemimah replied and Micah knew she had understood his reply the other way around. He bit into the chocolate again choosing not to explain himself, it was already more than enough that he had gone to these lengths to try to explain to her. His phone buzzed and Jemimah watched as lean fingers stretched out and pulled the phone out. He picked up the call and placed it on the loudspeaker.

"King" an unfamiliar voice rang out.

"Hmmm," King hummed in reply.

"Rain didn't fall but floods appeared" the latter muttered and Jemimah immediately frowned. What sense was that supposed to make but the next minute a small chuckle escaped Micah's lips. Jemimah glanced at her arm and her eyes widened upon realizing that the air on her arms was standing. The degree in the car had dropped a few degrees. She turned to him in shock and watched as his hand went to his neck adjusting it, she caught a glimpse of a tattoo on his neck but his hand was covering it so she couldn't see it well.

"Call Black, make the rain come," King said in a monotone and it took a second for Jemimah to realize that they were speaking using code words. She tried to think about what rain or floods could mean but something seemed to make sense. The call ended and King was still rubbing his neck.

"These people have a perfect way of annoying me" he whispered in the car and Jemimah immediately swallowed. King's hands dug into his pocket and immediately produced a pack of cigarettes, he was about to light one of them and paused before turning to Jemimah.

"You won't mind" he announced. He wasn't asking her not to mind, he was telling her there was nothing she could do about it. A small frown overtook Jemimah's features at his words.

"I just wanted to say thank you and it seems like you have something going on" Jemimah commented.

"So excuse me" Jemimah added not waiting for him to reply or bid good-bye, she opened the door and closed it behind her. A loud hiss escaped through her lips before she walked with a frown into the hostel.

———--

"With exams coming up in less than a month and CUA students still partying so hard, my initial impression of this school has been crushed," Doyin lamented, and Jemimah burst out laughing.

"They are like two perfect sides of a coin. "There is this girl in my depart-ment, I have no idea how I got her number, but she parties so hard," she admitted, shaking her head.

"I doubt there is a party going on, and you will not find her," she added, to which the other three burst out laughing.

"But guess what?" Jemimah asked, crossing her legs.

"She scored 30 or 27 out of 40 in all of the tests we had," she continued, and Peter laughed.

"Now that is some next-level shit," he said, and Jemimah nodded. "And she is not the only one, there is like ten other people like that and they did so well in their exams, beats me really," Jemimah added, shaking her head with a smile.

"Paul and one of those girls had the same score in BIO114, Paul has not even been to any party since he resumed," Jemimah revealed as Peter and Doyin burst out laughing.

"Why am I being used as an example?" Paul asked with a mock scowl on his face.

She answered, "You were the fastest I could think of," and the two started laughing again.

"Jemimah!" someone called, and Jemimah turned to see a very familiar face in front of her.

"Sarki?" she exclaimed, rising to her feet as the latter approached her.

"It is only been a short time since I last saw you, and you have gotten even prettier?" he asked, smiling, and Jemimah shook her head, amused.

"What are you doing at a first-year lecture theater?" she inquired.

"I am looking for you," Sarki replied, winking.

"As if," Jemimah retorted.

"I am about to hand something to someone, which reminds me, I was going to tell Bimbo to invite you since our paths have crossed, I am throwing a party tomorrow night, and I would like you to come," Sarki revealed, and Jemimah nodded.

"Oh wow, I will be there," she replied, smiling.

"You can come with your friends if you want." Sarki added, his gaze sweeping over the three others seated behind her.

Sarki went on, "And do not worry about how you are going to come; I will ask Black to pick you up." Jemimah nodded in agreement.

"Okay, okay," she said, giving him a firm handshake.

"See you," he said before sending flying kisses towards Jemimah. She laughed heartily as Sarki bolted from the classroom. She turned back to the three people who were seated behind her.

"And that reminds me, when were you three going to tell me that King was my brother's school father?" Jemimah inquired, and the three appeared to be frozen in their seats. Doyin stared at Jemimah in shock and shakily rose to her feet.

"Jemimah," Doyin said, and Jemimah sighed softly as she walked back to her seat.

'You see, the more I think about it, the more irritated and annoyed I become. When Paul and Peter told me about the Titians, I was terrified, and they conveniently left out the fact that my brother had something to do with them. That was not all; no one said anything about Black being the devil's right-hand man the day you guys saw him," Jemimah added. Her lips were pulled in a mocking smile as she turned to the twins.

"If you are wondering if I confronted him about what you guys said about him blowing people's heads off, the answer is that I did. So think hard and well before coming up with an explanation. If you are going to lie, consider my IQ first before speaking, and do not make stupid excuses."

The girl was smiling, but her eyes were cold and demeaning.

31 THIRTY ONE

J emimah leaned back, allowing Vickie to help her tighten the hold of her crop top. For the party, she had opted for a crop top once more, and Vickie was the one tying the knot because Doyin, Paul, and Peter still had not explained.

Deep down, she wondered what kind of excuse they would come up with - if they would lie to her or if they would tell the truth. Ever since she found out the truth, she has been having a hard time believing that her friends deliberately hid it from her.

They had not just hidden it from her; they had portrayed King and the Titians as murderers and bloodthirsty people. She had even sworn internally that she would run if she ever came across them. What were Paul and Peter thinking? What did they expect her reaction to be when she found out?

She had debated several times whether to bring it up with them or not and then the opportunity presented itself through Sarki. Remembering Doyin's shocked face and the twins' calm faces but anxious expressions made her have a headache. It was the first party ever that she was going to alone.

"Are you good?" Vickie asked with a small frown, tainting her pretty face. Jemimah responded quickly with a smile, "Yeah. I'm just bothered about something," she replied, picking up her small bag and stepping out of the room. Black had sent her a message minutes before saying that he was already outside the hostel.

She stopped quietly by the staircase while staring ahead. She didn't like that she was at loggerheads with her only friends but she didn't like it more that they hid such a piece of crucial information from her. She gulped lightly before continuing her descent down the stairs until she was outside the hostel.

"You look good," Black cooed as Jemimah entered the car, pulling her lips apart in a smile.

"When you say it like that, you are going to make me have second thoughts," she responded, causing Black to laugh.

"Might be funny, but even if you are only wearing a bikini, you will still be safe with me," he declared, and Jemima chuckled. "Why?" She asked.

"Because you are Jeremiah's sister, in a way that makes you my sister," Black replied with an amused smile on his lips, and Jemima nodded as she leaned into the car.

Murderers her feet.

"What's the courtesy for which Sarki is hosting a party?" She started a conversation the moment Black drove out of the school compound.

"Nothing. He just wants to have fun; that's the way he is. "He throws parties just because he wants to," Black said, his phone buzzing in his pocket. Leaving his left hand on the steering wheel, he allowed his right hand to delve into his pockets and bring out his phone. A smile spread across his lips as he glanced at his phone.

"Your brother is asking if I've picked you up." Black announced and Jemima nodded her head lightly while turning to stare at the streets shrouded in lights.

"Wait, are you guys not on speaking terms?" Black asked and Jemima chose not to reply.

She didn't know the exact answer to that question; after helping her out with Professor Farida's issue, they hadn't spoken again. Their relationship appeared to be on shaky ground; this had never happened before in their entire lives.

They had always been close since they were children; she was clingy to him, and Jeremiah adored his sister; he was the one person she was never afraid to be honest with, and she was the one person who understood him the best, despite the fact that he never explained himself. And now, their carefully cultivated relationship was on the verge of unraveling due to secrets that Jeremiah would rather keep hidden than reveal to her.

"There is nothing wrong with us; we both need a little time," she finally said, and Black looked at her with a serious expression. Jemimah turned to him and chuckled, "Yes. You are all partly to blame for what is going on with us, but do not worry, Jeremiah and I are the best siblings on the planet, and we will work it out," she said as Black drove into the club's premises.

The whole area was booming with music and the numerous cars parked around them told Jemimah that this was another huge party. She had underestimated Sarki's influence. She got out of the car and adjusted her earrings while Black led her through the door.

The party was even louder inside. Numerous young adults stuck to each other and filled the club with even more of the young adults with red cups, taking up the majority of the party. Her nose flared in displeasure at the smell of different scents in the air while she slowly followed Black upstairs.

"Jemimah," someone excitedly pulled her, and she turned to see Bimbo smiling at her. The latter had light makeup on her face that highlighted her features and even made her more attractive. She was clad in a skimpy gown that stopped just below her thoughts and a pair of heels graced her feet. Her hands dangled with silver bracelets and her fingers were curled around two different red cups.

"Hi, Bimmy," Jemimah said as she watched Bimbo quickly hand over the cups she was holding to someone else and pull her to the other side of the room.

"It's been so long since we last saw each other," Bimbo said, still grinding widely.

"Well, that is because you practically live at Jeremiah's," she responded, and Bimmy pouted, "You will not blame me on that one. How are you doing? How are the preparations for exams coming?" She asked and Bimbo shrugged.

"Quite alright, it's even crazier than we have less than two weeks to exam and I'm here to party," she replied and Bimbo burst into laughter.

"Oh, get used to it. Nobody knows who among Sarki and Hera throws the best parties. "Just have fun; that is their motto," Bimbo explained, and Jemimah laughed.

"And that reminds me, Bimbo, when were you going to tell me that my older brother, your boyfriend, was the school son of the leader of the deadliest cult in CUA?" She asked and Bimbo froze. Her grin vanished instantly, as if it never existed. She stared at Jemimah, blinking and gulping.

"Jemimah," she called, and Jemimah extended her hand to take a red cup from a passing waiter, gulping the contents and ignoring how bitter it was.

"If everyone lied to me, you shouldn't have Bimbo. I should not have found out from strangers what kind of identity my older brother has in CUA." Jemimah stated, "What excuse are you going to give me, Bimbo?" She continued speaking.

"Jemimah... I...." Bimbo found herself lost for words. She and Jeremiah had agreed to keep it a secret from Jemimah until the time was right. She never expected Jemimah to find out on her own, and Jeremiah has not informed her that she has found out. Spending their last year in secondary school together had allowed her to have access to Jemimah and know a few of her irks.

Making a fool out of her was one of the things Jemimah hated the most and while she had chided Hera for doing so, she had done the same thing to her.

"I was going to tell you when the time was right." Bimbo tried to defend herself and Jemima nodded, stretching her hand for another cup and downing the contents.

"Tell me, Bimbo, when is the right time?" She asked and Bimbo opened her mouth to reply but no words came out.

"You are all the same," she whispered as she walked away.

Jemimah didn't know anyone except Black, Bimbo, and her brother, and somehow she couldn't find Black and was on bad terms with both Bimbo and her brother. If only Doyin had followed her, she would have found someone to talk to, but they were on bad terms as well. But she was too engrossed in her thoughts and immediately jumped when an arm snaked around her waist and Jemimah whipped her head back in annoyance.

"Everyone had been looking over here, and it had made me wonder who the hell they were looking at; I should have known it was you," Sarki began, and Jemima chuckled as she removed Sarki's hand from her waist.

"I do not like people touching me," she explained, and Sarki nodded, "My apologies. I'm sorry," he replied and Jemimah smiled.

"Do not say the same thing as Black, please," she joked, causing Sarki to laugh.

"I have no idea what he said, but you are my sister, and I will not do anything to hurt you," he replied, and Jemimah rolled her eyes.

"Same thing, man, but with less gusto," she joked, and they both burst out laughing.

"Enjoying the party? Why are you alone?" Sarki asked two questions in rapid succession, which amused Jemimah.

"Yeah. Nice DJ, and your second question—why am I alone? I'm alone because everyone seems to be lying to me," Jemimah replied and Sarki's brows pulled together.

"Lying to you? What's the problem?" He asked with genuine concern in his eyes.

"Aren't you lying to me too? Aren't you a member of the Titans? The murderers?" Jemimah asked with a smile on her lips but Sarki burst into laughter.

"So that is what this is about," he said with a smile.

"Nobody lied to you, Jemimah; no one has the courage to lie to you, and no one needs to lie to you. If you asked a random stranger in CU, they would easily tell you who the Titians are; it is an open secret, and even the school administration is aware, so who is lying to you? Sarki asked with undisguised annoyance.

"So you've been going around trying to guilt trip everyone and make me feel like what for not telling you?" Sarki continued emptying his red cup and throwing it away.

"No one owes you anything here, Jemimah. You have no idea who we are, what we stand for, or why we do what we do; who the hell are you to criticize us and label us murderers?" He asked.

""Except for your brother, no one owes you anything. "Please get that entitlement off your head and open your damn eyes; this is CUA, and no one cares what you think about us," Sarki concluded.

"And just for your damn information, King is my best friend, but I am not a Titian," he revealed before walking away, a loud hiss escaping his lips.

Jemimah stood frozen in place, her highness and dizziness gone. She felt foolish because Sarki had dragged her out of her fantasy in the worst possible way. The only reason everyone else acted like they owed her something was because they cared about her.

"He's so right. You are so foolish. You don't deserve any explanation from them the way they don't deserve anything, even courtesy from you," she whispered to herself as she climbed the stairs.

"Have you seen Bimbo?" She asked one of the waiters, who immediately pointed out that Bimbo was seated among a set of girls she didn't recognize. Without another thought, she walked up to the seat and met Bimbo's gaze. "Bimbo, a minute please," she announced, silencing the entire table.

Bimbo gulped as she got to her feet and walked towards her.

"I want to apologize for my reaction earlier. I shouldn't blame you for anything; I shouldn't blame you for not telling me when I could have asked. My sense of entitlement slipped in again." Jemimah reeled off with a stoic face.

"Jemimah, don't..." Bimbo began, but Jemimah cut her off again. "Oh, I have to apologize," she said, and Bimbo sighed. She knew that Jemimah was irritated.

"Where can I find Black?" She asked and Bimbo pointed to the upper floor.

"Upstairs," she replied and Jemimah nodded, proceeding to climb the staircase but was immediately stopped by two bouncers.

"No one is allowed here," one of them said and Jemima was yet to reply when a voice transmitted over to them.

"What do you guys think you are doing? Let her in." The two bouncers immediately bowed in apology and let Jemimah in.

Jemimah glanced at the person who had spoken, Isa. Hera had her arm around his hand and was smiling at her; she had yet to open her mouth when Jemimah walked past them with no sense of gratitude.

Jemima's first sight was King at the bar table, surrounded by two other girls in even more skimpy gowns, chattering with a small smile on his face.

"Hey, Jemi," Black called, and Jemima turned to face him. "Oh, hello, I came to find you," she said, and Black furrowed his brow; he could sense the change of aura in Jemimah.

"Is there a problem?" He asked and Jemimah shook her head. "Not at all. I wanted to apologize." She started making Black's furrowed brows pull apart in irritation.

"What are you talking about?" he asked.

"Titians. You don't owe me an explanation; you don't owe me nada. Me going bonkers over it was so unnecessary," Jemimah replied and Black chuckled.

"Jemimah..." he began, but Jemimah interrupted him again. "Don't do that. King is busy right now so extend my apologies to him and Sarki. I'll do better by not expecting anything from you guys and I hope you guys keep it up by not expecting anything from me; there's nothing you could want from me anyway," Jemimah continued.

"The favor I owe King for Professor Farida's issue, I have repaid by not telling my parents what Jeremiah is involved in. "We are even that way," she concluded.

"Goodnight Black," Jemima said, turning and walking out of the club. Despite her blurry eyes, she managed to call an Uber while forcing back the tears tethering at the edge of her eyes.

******

King looked at Black calmly after he finished speaking, "She said that?" He asked and Black nodded.

"She needs to take a chill pill," Sarki said in irritation, and King turned to him with raised eyebrows. "Is that why you did the honors of giving her one?" He asked and Sarki returned to him with a frown.

"What do you mean?" he asked.

"You are correct, we do not owe her anything or an explanation, but it was not your place to tell her that; you are not a Titian," King responded, his words freezing everyone.

"Micah," Sarki called out, his voice hoarse.

"I do not care what you said to her; that is your business," he added, rising from his seat and walking away.

"Is he actually angry at me?" Sarki asked and Black chuckled.

"I doubt he is," he responded with a playful punch to Sarki's shoulders, "but you know he is right. Those words should have come out of your mouth at all."

32 THIRTY TWO

Annabelle furrowed her brows as she scrolled through her phone. There were several messages in the group but she had a hard time going through them. She rolled her eyes as she closed the chat window quickly.

Her coursemates were not just lousy in person, they were also lousy online, Every time she opened the group, there were always over 2000 messages unread. What was so interesting for them to keep talking about for hours?

She opened the Google Map, confirming that she was going in the right direction as she climbed the stairs. As for why her departmental president had asked for her, she had no idea. Her taciturn class president had sent her a message to visit the departmental secretariat because the departmental president wanted to see her.

Annabelle wondered if she had ever attended any departmental meeting or congress; most times she was too busy and other times she saw the information after the congress had been held. She had no friends in the department, not that she minded. So she certainly knew that she had never come across the president before. All efforts at guessing why her president would want to see her proved abortive.

Annabelle's eyes remained glued to her phone as she walked. Someone walked past her and her head was immediately whipped upwards as a smell drifted into her nose. The smell was sharp and refreshing, it made all the frayed nerves in her body cool down.

"Damn, you smell nice." Her lips parted to speak as she turned around to find out her voice had stopped the other person. A guy taller than her stood a few meters away from her, dressed in a casual round neck and free jeans and trousers, His oval face was attractive and the pair of blue-rimmed glasses resting on his small nose even further highlighted the attractiveness of his face.

"Excuse me?" He opened his mouth to say and Annabelle chuckled.

Nice smell. Nice voice.

"That's rare, for someone to tick the two boxes," Annabelle replied and the guy's full brows pulled together in confusion.

"Are you talking to me?" He asked again and Annabelle nodded.

"You smell like pine," Annabelle replied and the boy stared at her in surprise. He was yet to get out another word when Annabelle turned and walked away.

"It's the first time someone got it right, just by scent," he muttered into the air. He tilted his head, a puzzled expression crawling up his face, "She looks oddly familiar, who is she?"

DEPARTMENT OF PHARMACY

FACULTY OF MEDICAL SCIENCES SECTARIAT.

Annabelle glanced at the inscription inscribed on the wall and slowly stepped inside. A girl sat in the first seat, scrolling through her phone.

When she raised her head, Annabelle recognized her from a flash of surprise in her eyes.

"Hi, I'm here to see the President," Annabelle stated and the girl furrowed her brows.

"For?" For a brief moment, Annabelle thought she heard irritation in her voice.

"Well, maybe you should ask him, he asked for me," Annabelle said, and the girl looked at her incredulously for a moment.

Why would he send for you? What does he want from you?" She fired and Annabelle chuckled.

"I didn't mishear the first time," she replied and the girl frowned.

"Why don't you ask him all these questions you are asking me? My class president sent me a message informing me that the departmental president had asked me to come and see him. Annabelle added and the girl hissed loudly before standing up from her seat and walking further into the office.

Annabelle laughed as she sat down; she did not have time to indulge a fanatic. Her phone buzzed and Annabelle rubbed her glabella softly.

It was almost time again. Hopefully, it's less painful.

The girl strode out of the inner office and glared at Annabelle. "You can go in, but you can not use more than ten minutes," she said, and Annabelle met her gaze quietly. The girl shuddered as she found her seat.

Annabelle stood up and walked into the inner room, her fingers closed together and she knocked on the door.

"Come in," the crisp voice replied, raising Annabelle's brow as she turned the doorknob and entered the office. Her eyes flickered in surprise as she took in the office.

Student politicians sure enjoyed themselves.

The guy seated in front of her looked more mature than most guys she had seen in school, and he was handsome and looked somewhat presidential.

"Hello, Annabelle," he said, smiling, and Annabelle nodded, "Hi."

"I'm Okonkwo Jethro, current President of the Association of Pharmaceutical Students, CUA chapter. I'm in my fourth year," he introduced.

"Annabelle, first year," Annabelle replied, and Jethro laughed. "That's very concise," he noticed, and Annabelle raised her eyebrow at him.

"I don't like the way you are looking at me," he revealed, relaxing in his seat.

"I think I'm just very concerned about why you sent for me," Annabelle replied, and Jethro smiled.

"Well, it's come to my attention that you've never attended a faculty or departmental congress or meeting since you resumed; you've been absent from every one," Jethro started, and Annabelle furrowed her brows.

"I'm quite busy, and I always get the information late," she defended.

"It's compulsory, Anna. It affects your student's performance sheet at the end of the semester. I understand the position you hold; you are a model celebrity, and you have a full schedule. I just want to remind you that you are a student, and I need you to act like one," Jethro continued.

"None of your friends remind you when it's time for Congress?" He asked, and Annabelle stared at him, choosing not to reply. The smile on Jethro's face cracked as he laughed lightly.

"Don't tell me that almighty Annabelle, the number-six ranked teen model, is friendless," Jethro said, and Annabelle chuckled.

"I see you enjoyed that, but I have a friend. Yeah, just one, but she's not in my department. And I'd rather be a loner; I mean, I've always been a loner than be friends with those lousy girls," Annabelle replied, and Jethro burst into laughter again.

"Okay. Give me your number; my tenure ends when this semester ends, but there's one more Congress; I'll remind you," Jethro suggested, pushing his phone toward Annabelle.

"And I'll gladly be your second friend," he added, watching as Annabelle took the phone and pressed her number into it, pushing it back to him.

"Thank you very much, Jethro, but I don't need a second friend," she replied, standing up.

"Thank you," she added, and without waiting for Jethro's reply, she stepped out of the room. The girl sitting at the reception immediately jumped up as soon as Annabelle appeared.

"What did you guys talk about? What did you say to him?" She asked, eyeing Annabelle, and the latter chuckled.

"He doesn't like you. There's no way he likes nosy and insecure brats like you," she replied, and without allowing her to say another word, she walked out of the office.

Annabelle sighed softly as she walked away. She almost did not believe that not attending the faculty and departmental congress could have an impact on her student performance sheet. If there was anything wrong with her SPS, her manager would throw a fit.

Her phone started ringing, and a smile spread across her lips as she picked up the call.

"Heyy," she greeted. "You sound so cheerful," the latter replied sarcastically, and Annabelle burst into laughter.

"I just stepped out of my Departmental President's office," she explained. She could already imagine the latter's eyebrows pulling together.

"For what?" he asked.

"Apparently he found out I've not been attending departmental and faculty congresses. I said it could affect my student performance sheet," she replied.

"Oh, okay," he replied, and a minute of silence passed between the two of them.

"Are you okay? The nightmare's returned already." He asked, and Annabelle pursed her lips while nodding her head.

"Yeah. I couldn't sleep overnight," she replied, and the latter sighed.

"For now, just take your pills and call me whenever you can't sleep," he said softly, and Annabelle nodded.

"Ibukun isn't there?" She asked.

"Yeah. She went out to get something; she's worried about you too," he replied, and Annabelle smiled.

"I feel so proud for making Almighty Lashe and his girlfriend worry about me," Annabelle revealed, smiling, and Lashe chuckled.

"Who else would do the worrying?" He asked, and Annabelle could hear the laughter in his voice.

"Annabelle, take your drugs; I don't want anything to happen to you. Go to the hospital when it's time," he continued, and Annabelle nodded.

"Okay"

A few days ago, an important and very popular professor suddenly went on sabbatical without prior notice. Well, it was because she had bullied a female student of hers, namely J. J is a very popular first-year student with ties to a lot of people. Her coursemates had said Professor F had consistently humiliated J in front of the whole class by asking her questions that were outside the syllabus, even the ones she hadn't taught.

Determined to get rid of the bad blood, J had read extensively, answered the majority of Professor F's questions, and even attempted to see Professor F in her office several times, but it was futile as Professor F continued her onslaught in her classes.

J finally could not take it when Professor F marked her test script and gave her a zero, refusing to read her test answers even though they were clearly correct. Seeing the situation, a good samaritan took it upon himself or herself to report directly to the school authorities. I want you to take note that this good Samaritan is by no means an ordinary person because, overnight, Professor J was on a sabbatical and a new professor was assigned to them.

You can say luck was on J's side, and she celebrated by showing up to S's party and having the time of her life.

"We aren't idiots ButterFly Fairy, your use of alphabets has exposed the people you are talking about."

"I saw her at S's party yesterday; she looked so good."

"But what was Professor F's problem?"

"Well, someone said she was jealous that J was really pretty."

"Jealous? A full-blown adult?"

"I just want to know the Good Samaritan."

"Good Samaritan, my ass; we all know whose work this is."

"Do you have evidence? If I were you, I would keep my mouth shut."

"Leave her alone; when they come for her, she thinks she will find a Good Samaritan."

"By the way, J is a very patient person; I wouldn't even take this."

"Me too!"

33 | THIRTY THREE

J emima rubbed her forehead as she turned to face the wall. She scrolled slowly through the school forum with a blank expression on her face. ButterFly Fairy's post on the school forum had blown two days ago.

Vickie had shown it to her, the girls had gone on to insult ButterFly Fairy, and Jemima had been somewhat comforted. But she was getting irritated; this was the second or third time ButterFly Fairy had made a post about her; did she know her? From where did she get her information?

But Jemima had been unbothered. Fortunately for her, the students had supported her; otherwise, no one would have been able to stand the on-slaught of Professor Jemima. She closed the school forum and opened WhatsApp, staring at the unread messages without making a move to read or respond to them. There were four messages from Black, more than fifteen from Bimbo, and two from Jeremiah, and she made a firm decision not to respond to any of them.

A video call suddenly came in, and Jemima quickly sat up to accept it. A smile was quick to plaster itself on her lips as she waved at the camera.

"Hey, babe, what's up?" She greeted, and Sewa's voice filled the room.

"The first thing I saw was your fake smile," Adesewa responded, and Jemima burst out laughing. "I knew you would catch that. How are you?" She inquired, watching Sewa shrug through the camera.

"I am fine; I need to help my elder sister with something, so I will be flying to Minnesota in about four days," she said, and Jemima nodded silently.

"Can I talk?" Adesewa inquired, and Jemima quickly delved under her pillow, inserting her AirPods into her ears. The room was empty but the girls could walk into the room anytime; she couldn't risk that.

"Yes, you can," Jemima responded.

"It took a while, but I got some information on your girl, the Heraline girl," Adesewa said, beginning to move across her room.

"I sent them to your email, by the way. For a student, she does throw a lot of parties—lots of them. I mean parties where the La cream of your school attends. I hope you realize that your school is a beehive of celebrities; however, in comparison to Danish and Albert Macualy, your school is fairly normal. But every time she throws a party, the top people from your school come." She continued and Jemima nodded.

"You would not be lying to say that. I attended just one party and I saw that with my own eyes, there were plenty," Jemima replied.

"She also has affiliations with the guy I found the last time. King. Mann, I could barely find anything on him except one thing: You offend King in CUA; you are a dead man walking," Sewa revealed, making slashing movements around her throat.

"And I believe she sells drugs at her parties," Sewa stated solemnly, and Jemima frowned.

"Drugs?" She inquired, and Adesewa nodded. "I could not get much on that, but yes, drugs are being sold. Nobody knows who pays for it, she said.

"And I tried to see if I could connect anything from you to her but there was basically nothing. There are zero connections, so I can't even ascertain why she would specially invite you or why she would have wanted you at that party. There must be a reason why she wanted you there, but it has to be personal because even I cannot figure it out." Sewa continued to shake her head.

"And that makes it even weirder; I mean, her reason is personal; you two do not know each other, and this is not a soap opera where you met her when you were little," she added, causing Jemimah to laugh.

"After everything, Jemi, I only have one thing to tell you. You need to stay the fuck away from these people. They are dangerous, and they do not smell like trouble, Jemimah. They are trouble," Adesewa said, and Jemimah sighed.

"You came too late, Sewa; whatever I do now, I will still be embroided in whatever these people are doing. Jeremiah is King's school son." Jemimah dropped the bomb, and Adesewa stared at her mouth, agape.

"Are you joking right now, Jemima?" Adesewa asked and Jemimah shook her head.

"I wish I could. And then he hid it from me, Bimbo, as Doyin did. Paul and Peter even tried to find out if I knew by saying all kinds of things," Jemimah replied, and Adesewa furrowed her brow.

"Paul and Peter too? Why did they have to be that sneaky?" She wasked with irritation written all over her face and Jemimah shrugged.

"I hate that they hid it from me; they watched me express myself like a fool and laughed secretly at me. I found out because of you, and I was furious

until I confronted them; they refused to come clean about the situation."
Jemimah replied with pursed lips.

"We currently aren't on good terms because I demanded an explanation
from them. I'm scared that I'll lose the only friends I've made since I got
into CUA but I'm so mad that they treated me like that. It made me feel
like they did not treat me like a true friend," she admitted, sighing softly.

"No true friend would make you feel like this, Jemima, and I am not joking.
You have never avoided difficult conversations, and while most people
avoided you, I, Ing, and Farida remained because if there was a problem,
you would say it, which reduced our friendship problems and resentment,
and I loved it, and I still do." Adesewa was comforted, and Jemima smiled.

"I love it too. "You guys were the best ever," Jemima responded.

"What are you going to do, anyway?" Adesewa asked and Jemima shrugged.

"I think I'm going to have a discussion with Jeremiah; I need to know where
I stand in all of this mess. I absolutely cannot continue like this." Jemimah
responded by reaching a decision.

"What about Doyin, Paul, and Peter? For some reason, I don't feel good
about them doing this. I feel like they are going to come up with some
flimsy excuse to settle this issue." A

Sewa revealed her fears and Jemima nodded her head. "Do you want me to
look into Paul and Peter?" She asked and Jemimah immediately shook her
head.

"You do not have to do that," she said quickly. "I would rather be alone
than stick with people who tell me lies. I have no idea which parts of what
they have told me are true or false. What part is false and what is not?
Whatever they want with me, I'm going to find out. If they are going to

make a flimsy excuse, it better meet some standards," she added, causing Adesewa to laugh.

"It is fine; if you run into any problems, let me know." "I love you." Adesewa cooed, sending flying kisses through the screen.

"I love you too, Byeeee."

"Byeee"

Jemima allowed her back to fall slowly to her bed while closing her eyes. She was a little surprised at what Adesewa found.

Was Heraline also a member of the Titians? What did she want from her?

She tried to imagine if this was a soap opera; did she and Heraline meet when they were younger? Considering where Heraline lived and her history, there was no way they could have met.

Heraline wanted her at her party for some reason, and she needed to find out. Even if it meant getting involved with the Titians,.

There was a knock on the door and Jemima adjusted her laying posture. "Come on," she replied. The door opened and Doyin slowly walked in. Jemima maintained a blank expression as Doyin walked towards her.

"Can I sit down?" She asked and Jemima nodded, making space for her on the bed.

Doyin's eyes flickered back and forth in the room, resulting in a period of silence.

"I am sorry," she said, breaking the silence after nearly five minutes.

"Sorry for what?" Jemima asked and Doyin turned to meet her eyes.

"For hiding it from you. I didn't mean to hide it. I initially assumed you knew, as did Paul and Peter. We even expected you to bring it up in one of our conversations, but you did not." Doyin responded with a sincere look in her eyes.

"After a while, Paul realized you were unaware of the situation. Peter was convinced you knew and were just pretending, so they decided to question you in the hopes that you would finally admit you knew about it; who would have believed you did not know!" She exclaimed and Jemima nodded her head.

"Oh, okay," she replied softly.

Their excuse was pretty solid.

"I told them to let us tell you and fill you in, but Peter refused. He said if your brother or Bimbo did not tell you, it was for a reason and it was not our responsibility to tell you, and I agreed with them." Doyin continued, her voice becoming quieter.

"All the parts where Paul and Peter called King a murderer were made up. Paul and Peter have no idea who King or the Titians are; all we know about them is what we have heard from others," she added, attempting to dispel Jemimah's doubts.

"We did wrong. I made a mistake, and I sincerely apologize, Jemi. These past few days, I really hated myself and I almost can't believe that I hid it from you. I am deeply sorry; please forgive me." She finished wearing puppy eyes and Jemimah sighed softly.

"Next time, do not lie or keep things from me," Jemimah said, and Doyin nodded her head, placing her hand on her chest.

"I, Adedoyin, promise to never tell you, Jemimah, a lie again," she said under oath, and they both laughed. Doyin immediately wrapped her hands around Jemimah, hugging her.

"I have missed you so much," she cried.

"Me tooo," Jemima cried back, hugging Doyin.

"Let's go outside; Paul and Peter are waiting. They wanted me to apologize first before they did. "Said ladies first," Doyin said, and they both burst out laughing.

"Ladies first, my ass, cowards."